IN HER MOTHER'S SHADOW

IN HER MOTHER'S SHADOW

FAYE THOMPSON

URBAN BOOKS LLC
www.urbanbooks.net

Urban Books LLC
10 Brennan Place
Deer Park, NY 11729

ISBN 1-893196- 53-4

First Printing July 2006
Printed in the United States of America

10 9 8 7 6 5 4 3 2 1

This is a work of fiction. Any references or similarities to actual events, real people, living, or dead, or to real locales are intended to give the novel a sense of reality. Any similarity in other names, characters, places, and incidents is entirely coincidental.

Submit Wholesale Orders to:
Kensington Publishing Corp.
C/O Penguin Group (USA) Inc.
Attention: Order Processing
405 Murray Hill Parkway
East Rutherford, NJ 07073-2316
Phone: 1-800-526-0275
Fax: 1-800-227-9604

Acknowledgments

A dream fulfilled . . .

To the Center of My Joy & the Most High God: Thank you for pouring out my blessings and revealing to my soul that I'm a child of the King.

Dorothy J. Peat: You loved me before I even learned to love myself. Whew!!! We've been through so much together, and yet, we can still smile. Your eyes really do sparkle when I enter the room, and my heart rejoices because of it.

Daniel Hill: You taught me how to survive, and for that alone I will always honor you. Now you're up there working things out for me—from your lips to God's ears . . . And the beauty of it all is that He's listening!

Hubert & Novella Thompson, William & Alma Hill, Aunt Mae, Aunt Martha Lee, Aunt Lizzie, Uncle William C: This one's for you!

Uncle Amos & Aunt Maxine: You make me proud to be a Thompson.

Aunt Marjorie & Dawna Michelle Fields: How can I ever thank you for Paris?

Doloris Brown, Louise Hines: You are constant reminders that, yes, with God ALL things are possible.

Elder Del P. Shields: You've been with me during the lowest points of my life as well as my proudest moments. Thank you for believing in me. Please keep me in your prayers.

Mama Eloise Sealy: You are priceless!!!

Cinderella Newman of When We Were Queens: We truly were sisters in another lifetime.

Lynette Clark: When I walked in you told me I was dripping in pearls. But if the truth be told, you're the one dripping in pearls—of wisdom!

Howard J. White: These past few years have been positively amazing. You help keep me grounded and focused. Thank you for being such a wonderful part of my life.

To Carl Weber, Roy Glenn, and my editor Chandra Sparks Taylor: Thank you for taking me under your wings and bringing me into your inner circle.

Special thanks to James Ricca, counselor at law.

And finally, to my readers: Please be patient with me. God is not through with me yet.

Enjoy the read!

"A half truth is a whole lie."
—Yiddish Proverb

Chapter 1

Bronze Sutton breathed in the fresh May air as she set out for lunch. She loved the feeling of the sun on her golden-brown skin, or as her last customer said, her café au lait complexion. She was by no means vain yet quite beautiful with her green eyes and brown hair, which gently grazed her shoulders. She was often reminded of her beauty by a variety of leering men; its effect on them never ceased to amaze her. In fact, there were days she was tempted to stop wearing makeup to avoid all the catcalls and compliments. But this was not one of those days. Today she accepted her beauty.

She loved working at the Fragrance Bar in Hubert's Northeast department store, though the pay left something to be desired. But after being laid off from the bank, she was grateful that what started out as a part-time job at the store turned into a full-time position. With the current state of the economy and so many people out of work, she felt quite lucky even though she could hear her mother's voice saying that she was not lucky, but instead blessed. Luck was just a four letter word. Bronze had to agree. Someone up there was definitely looking out for her.

By the time she joined her coworkers for a bite to eat in the mall's food court, they were casting their opinionated votes about who would head the Velvet line of cosmetics at the new Hubert's set to open that summer in Middle Heights, Ohio.

"Rashelle has it in the bag. I mean, she's been Velvet's assistant line girl for what, five years? That has to count for something. Her name's written all over it," Dawn Daley from Prescriptives insisted.

"Get real!" Lancome's Liz Tangiano was the only white girl in the group. "M&Ms will replace the pill before she gets promoted! Maybe if she knew how to make it to work on time she would have a better chance," she commented just before biting into a slice of pizza.

"Ooh, have you heard the latest?" Monique Hall from Fashion Fair didn't wait for an answer but lowered her voice to a whisper. "Amanda has a baby in layaway. That's why she left. Honey, ain't no sick aunt in Detroit." Only Monique pronounced it *De-twah*.

"Get outta here." Bronze was surprised.

"Not only that, but guess who's the father? Steve from Electronics; that brother has some strong stuff; you hear me? A sister can just look at him, and she's pregnant."

"Didn't Nadine just have his baby?" Liz asked.

"Yeah, this makes the third one. They are supposed to be getting married, but I wouldn't have his cheatin' behind for nothing." Dawn added.

"Well, then, Steve needs to stop eating so many freakin' carrots, because he's spitting kids out like a bunny rabbit," Monique said and they all burst into laughter. "Wasn't he trying to talk to you a couple of months ago?" she asked Dawn.

"Yep, then called me out of my name when I wouldn't give up the digits. He gets nothing here. All this boom-shocka-locka," Dawn cut her eyes over her shoulder to reference her rounded behind, "is for my baby."

"Girrrl . . ." Monique laughed, "I'm scared of you!"

"Anyway, I hope you put in for the position, Bronze," Liz said, bringing the subject back to the promotion opportunity.

"Sure did; I'd love to pioneer a launch. That will do wonders for my career."

"I know what you mean."

"You guys will never guess what I saw last night on cable," Monique said smiling. "*Jason's Lyric.*"

"Not again? Why don't you just buy the DVD?" Liz asked.

"Yeah. Then I could decide when to sweat out my perm." Monique grinned, fanning herself with a flimsy napkin. "That Allen Payne is hot. Why do you think I'm wearing braids today? I don't know why Hollywood won't give a brother more play. You know what they say; no Payne, no gain."

The ladies finished up their lunches, cleaned off the table and hurried back to Hubert's.

The remainder of the afternoon went well for Bronze. The store was extremely busy, making for good sales. In addition, she'd sold every single bottle of Spontaneous—the brand new fragrance by designer Marc Underwood, with the last four from her inventory going to a gentleman who was out shopping with his four daughters. The girls looked to be in their late teens—early twenties, and each carried several shopping bags from a variety of stores. The father, with his peppery well-groomed hair and broad shoulders, looked a bit exasperated but seemed to be thoroughly enjoying his daughters spending his money.

The girls had wandered over to a nearby jewelry counter leaving the father at Bronze's counter alone. He sprayed the air with the fragrance, waited a few seconds, then spoke nonchalantly. "I'll take four of these." Bronze rang up the transaction and placed each item neatly in a gift bag, as she fought back tears. She desperately longed for her father, wanting to be in his presence and enjoy a day of shopping, or even a simple conversation.

"Dad, why'd you get us all the same thing," the younger one whined returning to her father's side.

"Because I love you all the same, princess," he replied handing his credit card to Bronze. "You girls have been picking what you wanted all day; can I pick something I want you to have?" He kissed the girl on her forehead, and then focused his attention to the jewelry counter where he was being beckoned to look at a charm bracelet.

Somehow Bronze completed the transaction without crying, though her hands trembled so much that the gentleman asked if she was okay.

"Oh, yes. I'm fine; I just need to eat a little something, that's all," she lied. Sadly, the truth was, Bronze's father was a man she'd never known. She generally could ignore that fact, as well as overlook the pain she buried along with it, but every once in a while it would buoy into her consciousness, and she'd be forced to deal with it—like today. She remembered her fifth birthday as though it were only yesterday. That was the day she promised herself to never ask her mother about her daddy again. The way her mother broke down and cried upon her asking where was her daddy, was simply too much for Bronze to comprehend and swallow. Her mother cried so profusely, Bronze felt guilty for even asking. In twenty years she hadn't broken that promise. But there was so much she didn't know and didn't understand. . . .

Later that evening after closing, the storeowner Lynn Hubert herself called Bronze into her office. Vonnie Redman, the cosmetics manager, was also there. Bronze's first thought was, *Okay, what's up*? Lynn gestured for her to have a seat.

"Bronze," she began, "let me get straight to the point. I've watched you out on the sales floor, and you impress me. You're an asset to Cosmetics, and your customers love you." She stopped and smiled, displaying even pearly whites. "The grand opening of the new Hubert's is next month—if things go as scheduled, that is. Anyway, I know you know the Fragrance Bar like the back of your hand, but I want you to head the Velvet line. I think your presence there would be a tremendous asset." She paused to interpret Bronze's wide-eyed facial expression. "How about it?"

"I'd love to." Bronze tried to hide her excitement by folding her hands in her lap, but her eyes and voice tone said it all.

"Great!" Vonnie said. "Now, we're going to have to ask you to keep this under wraps until we've had an opportunity to talk to all of the other applicants. There were nearly fifty other associates who had their eyes on this prize."

"Rashelle will have a fit," Bronze said.

"Let me give you some advice, Bronze. I'm not saying be a bitch, but in this business, you have to look out for number one. Rashelle will get over it, and there will be other promotions. You deserve this one. End of story." Lynn was frank.

Bronze thanked both women for their confidence in her and promised them that they would not be disappointed. She headed home, eager to share the news of her promotion with her mother.

Stephanie Sutton could have easily passed for Bronze's older sister with her thick, brown hair, which was just beginning to gray, but her daughter needed a mother and she took her rightful place as such. She was a few inches shorter than Bronze, but never let her forget that she was the mother.

"Guess what happened at work today?" Bronze slid out of her suit jacket and laid it across the back of the sofa.

"What?" Stephanie glanced up from the magazine she was reading.

"I got the promotion. Rashelle is gonna have a fit. She's the one who got me the job at Hubert's in the first place."

"Yes, I remember."

"Everyone was thinking she had it all wrapped up."

"Don't worry about Rashelle, and don't let her steal your joy. You just got a promotion. Congratulations to you; you deserve it so be happy." Stephanie rose from her chair and sauntered into the kitchen to get a mini second serving of the meal she'd prepared. "I made salmon cakes. Are you hungry?"

"Nah." Bronze waved the notion of dinner away with her hand. "Well, it looks like another dateless Friday night."

"By choice," Stephanie added. "Bronze, you're

twenty-five years old. You're beautiful, intelligent, and you have a lot going for you. You should be out there enjoying life, not home baby-sitting me. What's wrong with Jerome? He's nice, and you know he likes you. Give him a call."

"Jerome?" Bronze crinkled her nose at the very thought of the unkempt man. He made a pretty decent living as the owner of a janitorial business, but only because his brother Frank did his bidding for him. Jerome always looked like he'd fallen out of bed during a nightmare. "Ma, that man doesn't even comb his hair! And he probably doesn't own an iron. No thank you!" she retorted.

"You don't have to be in love with someone to go out." She spooned a small helping of store-bought potato salad that she'd doctored up with a little onion powder, relish and hard-boiled egg onto a plate along side of a salmon cake.

"I know that, Ma, but can we at least go for remotely attracted to? Jerome is just not my type." Bronze picked a fork from the dish rack and dabbled in her mother's plate while Stephanie's back was turned to pour a glass of iced tea.

Glancing over her shoulder, Stephanie caught a glimpse of her daughter's hand rising to her mouth. "Girl, don't make me pop you! There's another plate in the cabinet and there's food in the fridge. I just asked you if you wanted some and you said no," she said laughing while snatching her plate away. "Not your type, huh? You don't even know yourself what your type is."

"Maybe not," Bronze licked at her fork, "but when I meet him I'll know."

Chapter 2

Ordinarily, Bronze hated mornings, thus had a horrid time rising each day. In fact, the harder the dawning sun flirted at getting her attention, the more she chose to ignore it by hiding under the covers. The only thing that kept her from doing so today was her excitement about the two-day training session for the Velvet line. The grand opening of Hubert's in Middle Heights was an event that Bronze eagerly anticipated.

She woke with a start, showered, and slipped into a pair of white slacks and a peach silk top. In minutes she had applied a little shadow to her eyelids and coated her lips with Velvet's Copper lipstick. With a few hairpins, her tresses were secured into a chignon, then she further accented her facial features with a pair of pastel seashell earrings. Her reflection in the full-length mirror confirmed that she was stylish, presentable and ready for her day. She gulped down a glass of orange juice and was out of the door with Stephanie, who'd agreed to drop her off at the train station on her way to work. As she walked to the car,

Bronze stopped and inhaled deeply, appreciating the warmth of the sun and the liveliness of the season.

Bronze was a summer person; she looked forward to it all year because she found summer the most invigorating of all seasons. Just breathing in the fragrant air gave her a rush, which she referred to as her summer high. Summer was the strongest aphrodisiac.

Arriving at the hotel, Bronze was pleased to see a conference room full of well-dressed, skilled and proficient African-Americans. She noticed that there was even one male in the group. This collaboration of professionals reminded Bronze of her senior year in high school when she wrestled with the idea of attending a black college. Reality, as she saw it, prevailed when she decided that it was best not to be lulled by a false sense of security, only to have one's self pricked awake later by a white world. In the end she attended Ohio University and graduated with a degree in marketing. Sometimes she wondered if she had made the right decision.

Bronze scanned the registration table for her name badge and packaged materials, then was ushered into one of the hotel's conference rooms by the training instructor, a middle-aged, chestnut-colored petite woman named Joanne Price. Joanne introduced a taller, younger woman as her assistant. Marlene Johnson looked to be in her early to mid-thirties. Bronze assessed the two women standing before her. They weren't drop-dead gorgeous, but they both could have easily passed for models. Both had good bone structure and knew their stuff when it came to applying makeup.

"Well, let's start out first by going around and having everyone introduce themselves and tell us all something about themselves," Joanne began.

The stud, if he could be called that, was Julian Mitchell. Naturally, as the sole male in the group, he stood out like a yellow highlighter, but he didn't appear the least bit uncomfortable in that role. On the contrary, he seemed to enjoy all the stares and smiles that were aimed in his direction. In fact, he openly flirted with some of the women who were a bit forward. Bronze was immediately turned off. He was probably just a big player.

He appeared to be slightly older than Bronze, and from where he sat across from her at the large oval oak conference table, she noticed that his nails were short and square. Hands were the second thing she noticed on a man, whether or not she was attracted to him. And in this case she obviously was not, she decided. Eyes were the first things of which she took stock. His were a soft brown protected by long, sexy lashes and dark eyebrows. Funny, his eyes reminded Bronze of melted milk chocolate—warm and smooth. Julian felt her eyes upon him and turned to meet her gaze. Bronze was the first to look away, rolling her eyes to make a point.

Bronze appreciated the fact that one of the girls she currently worked with, Deandra Kay, would be her part-time assistant in Middle Heights. She seemed friendly, and one friendly face was better than none.

"When I first started out with Velvet," Joanne paused, "there were nine shades of lipstick and matching nail polish that I had to memorize, so you know how long ago that was! But today with forty-three shades, it's much more challenging." She stressed the word *much*. "The cosmetics industry has experienced a color explosion in the last few years. Women are making their color needs known and expect them to be met. Color not only affects the wearer, but the observer as well. It influences our moods. It's a powerful tool, and women are learning to use it to their advantage."

As the morning progressed they learned about Velvet cosmetics from its conception twenty-seven years earlier by Eileen Harris, to the present. Madame H believed that there was room for another black cosmetics company besides Flori Roberts and Fashion Fair. Most people didn't know that Flori Roberts was a white woman. Velvet was quickly gaining momentum as the makeup choice for Generation X, whereas Flori Roberts and Fashion Fair were geared towards the older set.

Madame H started the company with her life savings—two thousand dollars—and a whopping dose of faith. She couldn't even get a bank loan. In those days a loan to a single, black woman was virtually unheard of. With the aid of a local businessman who needed a tax break and much hard work and determination, she was able to build Velvet into a multimillion-dollar entity.

Bronze admired Joanne and Marlene for the confidence they exuded in managing the class. Had her mother been present, she would have reminded Bronze that the two instructors were just doing their jobs and that almost anything could be learned—even rapport and confidence.

They all sat through another hour of lecture before breaking for lunch.

Bronze was not surprised when Julian Mitchell approached her as the group headed for the dining area. Perhaps he was in the mood for a challenge. Standing beside him she realized how tall he was. But then at five feet four inches, Bronze never had a problem finding tall men. Julian fell into step with her much to the dismay of some of the other women who openly rolled their eyes.

They walked the short distance to the dining room where a buffet awaited them. The four large, round tables, covered with white tablecloths and topped with fresh-cut lilac carnations adorned with baby breath, easily accommodated the group.

Bronze and Julian fixed their plates and found seats. She noticed that he removed the skin from his baked chicken and ate plenty of garden salad—further justification for his lean six-foot, one-inch frame. She, on the other hand, had a generous portion of lasagna. When her stomach talked she listened, simple as that.

"So, Bronze," he confirmed reading her name badge. "Do you get out to this part of town much?" he asked.

"No."

"How's the lasagna?"

"Fine."

"You're as talkative as a pet rock."

"Look, I'm just trying to enjoy my meal, not trying to date you."

"Don't flatter yourself, Miss Thang. I'm hardly after a date with you either sweetheart. It's called friendly conversation. You know, you pretty girls tickle me. Somebody says hello to you, and right away you think they wanna jump your bones. Get over yourself." Julian stood to his feet, grabbed his plate and went to sit with a more welcoming group of ladies. Bronze looked over at a neighboring table where about seven other women sat snickering. She was certain that they had heard every word of the conversation. Their outburst of laughter accommodated with snapping fingers in mid air gave them away. Too embarrassed to move or respond, she ate the rest of her meal alone and in silence, attempting to hold her head up despite the heat she felt rising to her cheeks.

That afternoon Joanne and Marlene introduced Velvet's new summer collection, which included colors like Paprika Passion and Smashing Melon. Bronze was eager to learn all she could about Velvet's skin-care line as she used it herself. She made it a part of her daily ritual from the cleanser and toner to the freshly scented Vitamin E enriched moisturizer.

Marlene and Joanne also provided helpful hints on applying blush. It was the general consensus that powdered blush was easier to control than cream. Even Julian had to agree. "From a makeup artist's point of view, of course," he quipped. They all laughed with the exception of Bronze; she was not amused.

The clock read five 'til five when the facilitators called it a day. Bronze gathered her purse and other belongings, anxious to become reacquainted with the May sunshine. Not only that, but she did not want another embarrassing scene with Julian Mitchell. She walked out of the lobby, filling her nostrils with the smell of summer's nectar, its fragrance causing her senses to tingle. She noticed a mimosa tree just starting to bloom whose outstretched branches seemed to beckon her to it for no other reason than to say enjoy the moment. Carpe diem.

Later that evening Bronze and Stephanie filled each other in over dinner on how their days went. Stephanie's day as a first-grade teacher went well. School was nearly out for the summer, and this had been Awards Day. Stephanie made certain that each of her nineteen students received an award whether it was for most improved, best attendance, or most imaginative. She believed in boosting her pupils' self-esteem and making them all feel special rather than pitting one against the other and fostering excessive competition. As a result, she was a favorite with the students as well as with the parents and faculty.

"So, how was your day?" Stephanie asked her daughter.

"Interesting."

"That must mean you met someone." Stephanie raised one inquisitive brow.

"Yeah. I met this guy named Julian." Bronze folded her lips inside her mouth as she imagined what it must be like to have Julian hold her from behind and nibble on her neck.

"And?"

"And he's gorgeous."

Stephanie caught a glint of naughtiness in her daughter's eyes. "But?" she asked, sensing there was something more.

"But I think he's just a big player," Bronze huffed in disappointment. There was a slight pause before Stephanie's response.

"Well, I would hope that you learned your lesson after being involved with Carlon, but you sound as if you're interested."

Bronze sucked at her teeth and rolled her eyes upwards. "Puhleez. He already thinks he's God's gift to women. I don't have time for that."

"I hope not. I almost forgot," Stephanie said. "I picked up cannolis on the way home."

"Thanks, Ma. You always think of me." Having already slipped out of her heeled sandals, Bronze's naked toes kissed the cool, white linoleum as she headed over to the counter and returned with the familiar, wax-covered bag filled with her favorite pastry. She had already taken one big bite, the white cream covering her full lips, before Stephanie had taken her cannoli out of the bag.

"Mmmm. Nobody makes cannolis like *Oooh Cannolis*, huh?"

"Delicious," Stephanie agreed.

"I think I better stop while I'm ahead." Bronze knew that she could easily eat the entire bag. She wiped the corners of her mouth and offered to do the dishes.

"Thanks, hon. I'm beat. I think I'll turn in early tonight." Stephanie placed her dishes in the sink and headed for her bedroom. "And don't you lay up in bed tonight thinking about that player," she warned, but left the room before Bronze could give a reply.

As Bronze cleared the table and cleaned up the kitchen, she couldn't help but entertain the thought of Julian, if only for a few minutes. There was something about him beyond sexy and beyond intriguing. In addition to whip appeal, Julian had mad flex appeal. He had what it took to make her privately flex her muscles over and over again, sometimes involuntarily. She looked around at the kitchen with its daisy border along the top of sunny yellow walls. She placed the chairs neatly underneath the square butcher-block table and put the leftovers in the fridge, still thinking about her attraction to this man. She couldn't quite explain why she wanted to catch his eye, but the idea excited her nonetheless.

At 9:30, she headed to her bedroom, deciding to wash her hair and select her clothes for the next day. She laid out a shrimp-colored linen sheath with matching stilettos, although she knew by the end of the day she would regret her shoe selection. She chose hanging silver earrings along with a matching pendant necklace that said sophistication and elegance. She wanted to glam up for the last day of the seminar, and if Julian noticed, so much the better.

When she put the finishing touches on her make-up the next morning, she knew that she would turn heads, Julian's in particular. Again she couldn't explain why she wanted to be flirtatious with a player. It really didn't make much sense, especially after the way she had been burned by Carlon.

Carlon Maurice Jones was the man to whom she had given her virginity. The bum. He had gotten not one, but two girls pregnant during the three years they were together. Talk about working overtime. When her best friend, Angela, broke the news to her, Bronze felt as though someone had ripped out her heart. She didn't believe it at first, couldn't believe it. Carlon would never betray their love for each other. But when both girls came to her with a description of the boot-shaped birthmark on his butt, it could be nothing else but true.

Without hesitation, she severed the relationship, and in her quest for the perfect relationship, adopted the three G's: look good, smell good, and treat me good. But experience had taught her that if a man had any two G's, he usually lacked the third. Which was really a tragedy. There were so many two-legged dogs. She often wondered if the odds were stacked against her.

Being so engrossed in her thoughts, Bronze nearly missed her stop. She got off the train, trotted down the steps, and began the short walk to the hotel.

The lobby was relatively empty except for a few businessmen by the checkout desk. She checked her watch as she took the elevator to the mezzanine floor and strolled towards the meeting room. As she approached a long table set with continental breakfast foods, she took a moment to sling both her purse and messenger bag on to her back, in order to grab a prepackaged banana nut muffin and a sealed cup of juice. Joanne and Marlene stood like sentinels in the doorway greeting each participant as they entered the room, and checking names off of their rosters.

"Good morning!" Joanne sang in her most chipper facilitator voice. "We've done a little shuffle with the seating today, so you may have to hunt around for your name tent," she added. Bronze put on her brightest smile.

"Great! I was hoping for the opportunity to network with a few others from the Bridge Crossing location. Maybe they can share their secrets on how to maximize sales for those little striped wrist bands we got in to match the new lip colors; I heard they've moved them all."

"Yeah, I'm sure Chrissy would be glad to tell you what they're doing. I can't promise you that you'll be seated by her though," Marlene winked and let her voice trail off as if to say *don't get your hopes up!*

It took Bronze a minute to locate her name tent, but soon found her seat next to Deandra. Glancing at the tent on the other side of her sent a flutter through her system. She would be sitting beside Julian. By sheer reflex, she jerked her head around to see if he was coming through the door, but there was no sign of him. It was only 8:45; Julian still had a good fifteen minutes before the class started.

"Hey girl," Deandra welcomed, kindly taking Bronze's juice from her hand and sitting it on the table while Bronze settled into place. "I'm ready to get started 'cause the sooner we start, the sooner we can leave. Looks like just about everyone is here."

Bronze nodded and smiled. *All except Julian,* she thought. A few minutes after nine, she caught herself glancing at her watch and inconspicuously watching the door. Where in the world could he be? Perhaps he intended to make a grand late entrance as if being the only male in a group of thirty women wasn't enough.

At each place setting around the table were several shades of foundation, cheek color, eye shadow, and lip color, as well as applicators all arranged on a clear, plastic sixteen-by-twenty sketch of a woman's face. In the center of each table were two large wicker baskets holding an assortment of cosmetics in various shades.

"Today, Marlene and I will be discussing application," Joanne began. "We want each of you to partner with a neighbor, and we'll get started. Since the biggest part of your job at Velvet is assisting women in selecting the most flattering cosmetics, they will benefit most from a rep that stays on top of her business. Notice I said assisting. Never pressure a customer into purchasing something she's not completely comfortable with, no matter how good it may look on her. I cannot stress this enough. On the other hand, if she feels that she looks absolutely striking in that bright red lipstick she's wearing and you know she looks like a blood-sucking hyena with it on, suggest a more flattering shade. Be tactful. Remember, you want to build rapport with your customers. And another thing to keep in mind is that cosmetics and fragrances are affordable luxuries. They're mood alterers, therapy in a bottle."

While Deandra and Bronze practiced the new application techniques on sketch after sketch, Bronze stole another glance at her watch. She found herself getting frustrated by Julian's absence, although she had no right to be. Everyone else seemed to be captivated by what the instructors were saying, but Bronze was too busy thinking about Julian's caramel complexion and soulful eyes. She shook her thoughts, telling herself that he didn't matter to her. After all, they had just met. Not only that, but what could another player do for her? She didn't need him to complicate her life. She forced her attention to the instructors.

Finally, right before noon, an apologetic Julian strolled in complaining of car trouble. He looked as if he had just come from a Fine Black Man convention, sporting a beige suit with mocha brown accents. With his suit coat draped over his index finger and down his back, Bronze could almost swear she heard the click and whir of a photographer's camera. There was no need for a flash; Julian's teeth took care of that as he grinned at a Latino chick who raised her eyebrows and puckered her lips letting him know that she'd take him on if she caught him by himself. Bronze, though secretly thrilled to see him, didn't so much as crack a smile when he looked in her direction. She refused to make a public spectacle of herself.

Julian had barely sat down before the training session broke for lunch. During that hour, several from the group, Julian included, decided to get together for drinks after class. Bronze would have just as soon skipped it, but Deandra talked her into it.

"Come on; it'll be fun," Deandra insisted. "What is it that you have to do after work that is preventing you from saying yes? Read email or something?" After a few seconds of thought, knowing that her evening would probably be nothing more than watching sitcom reruns over a chicken salad sandwich and a few potato chips, she figured she had nothing to lose . . . plus it would afford her a little off-the-clock face time with Julian.

"Okay," Bronze nodded. "Count me in."

The rest of the afternoon couldn't have gone by any slower. The upbeat voices that greeted the class that morning seemed to have become drained and monotonous, reminding Bronze of the man from the eye drop commercials. She shifted in her chair slightly in an attempt to wake herself a little. When her leg bumped Julian's under the table it sent a tremor from her kneecap up her thigh and to her secret place.

"Excuse me," she whispered. Julian gave a quick wink in response. And although no one noticed, the wetness she immediately felt in her panties embarrassed her.

Certain that the class would all uphold the Velvet standard and reputation and make Madame H proud, Joanne and Marlene concluded the seminar a few hours later. They distributed a large gift basket filled with spa treats to each participant, then wished them all success in their home stores.

There were a total of eight that decided to hang out after work, and gathered in a small circle at the hotel's entrance to wait for each other. While Joanne and Marlene had been invited, they declined the offer, needing to get on the road. Julian, in true gentleman fashion, helped the two ladies load their training paraphernalia into their rented car, and then led the way to a nearby supper club, *The Blox,* which was within walking distance from the hotel. Since it was just 5:30, the after-work crowd hadn't yet arrived, and they could all be seated at one large table.

Two waitresses came over to get drink and appetizer orders while small talk about the training crossed the table. Julian, who sat across from Bronze, seemed to be in a deep conversation with the girl to his left, intentionally keeping his volume low as not to be overheard. At one point he gently touched her hand to make a point, and she threw back her head and laughed. It was obvious that they were flirting with each other. Then, Julian asked her to dance, and they both stood and walked over to the dance floor.

Bronze sipped her mudslide and wondered what he could possibly see in his dance partner. She wasn't much to look at, unless he liked bones. She was no bigger than Bronze's pinky finger with a head full of micro-braided weave. With her long toothpick-like legs growing from under her pleated mini-skirt, she looked like a damn umbrella. And that hoochie Gucci wear made her look like the freak of the week. Once out on the dance floor, she really showed just how much of a hoochie and freak she was, unashamedly bouncing her booty, what little she had, up against Julian. Bronze was appalled . . . and jealous.

The small club suddenly became more crowded. The waitress pushed her way through a number of patrons, approaching the table with a new round of drinks and a platter of hot wings, just as Julian and his dance partner returned to the table laughing. Before the wings hit the table, a small cup of blue cheese dressing slipped from the edge of the platter and fell right onto Bronze's lap, forcing her to the ladies' room, trailed by the waitress's apologies. After ten minutes of wiping, rinsing, scrubbing, and standing under the hand dryer, Bronze was thoroughly pissed. Then to top it off, when she returned, Julian was on the dance floor with not one, but two girls. That's when Bronze decided that she couldn't stand him. Sandwiched between the two, he gyrated his hips to R. Kelly's *Ignition;* it was obvious that he had no complaints. She watched in disgust while he sang the words to both girls as if he were the R & B artist himself. Apparently, he thought he was a prize. He was nothing but an arrogant piece of crap.

I don't need this! Bronze thought. She was totally repulsed and sorry that she had wasted the evening, not to mention the cost of having to dry-clean her dress. Bronze said her good-byes. She fumbled in her purse for enough money to cover the cost of her drink and appetizer, placed the bills on the table, and walked out the door without as much as a backwards glance at Julian Mitchell.

Chapter 3

Work had been incredibly hectic with grand opening preparations, but Bronze was able to settle into a comfortable routine. She worked five days a week at Hubert's Northeast, including one night. Sure, it was tiring standing on her feet all day, but overall Bronze enjoyed her work. What she loved most was the fact that after she left the store, her time was her own. There was never any stress or paperwork to take home.

Her only regret was the time, energy, and money spent on college. Had it all been in vain? After all, one certainly didn't need a bachelor's degree to work in a department store. But then again, Bronze did not intend to be a salesclerk all her life. Maybe one day her college background would be utilized.

It had been two weeks since the beauty seminar, and though she thought about Julian occasionally, her memory of him was indeed beginning to fade. They had only interacted those two days; it wasn't as if he was the love of her life.

Stephanie was relieved to know that her daughter's interaction with Julian had ceased. Bronze had too much going for herself to get involved with a man who could only bring her heartache and sorrow. Thank God things had worked out for the best.

From the moment Bronze got behind the Velvet counter at Hubert's that morning, she knew she was in for a hectic day. Instead of reporting to Middle Heights for more prep work, she was asked to report to her old store to cover for someone who had called in at the last minute. A new shipment of Velvet's summer collection had just arrived, and Bronze had barely enough time to replenish the existing stock before eager customers devoured it like kids, wolfing down homemade cookies. It appeared that the Precious Cantaloupe and Perfectly Sassy Fuchsia lipsticks and nail polishes would be the big sellers that summer. Velvet was a popular line to begin with, but when it offered GWPs—gifts with purchase—as they were doing while supplies lasted, a deluge of women found themselves at the Velvet counter. This GWP included a moisturizer, mascara, lipstick, and a purse-size bottle of Bliss eau de toilette spray.

By the time her lunch hour rolled around, Bronze welcomed the break. She and Monique joined Liz and Dawn, who were already at Ooh Cannolis. They walked into the brightly lit restaurant with its red-and-white checkered tablecloths. Famous for its bakery, Ooh Cannolis was a favorite with the mall crowd.

"So what's up for tonight, Bronze?" Monique was curious.

"Ebony's with Angela. Wanna join us?" she replied.

"No, I gotta work late tonight, and I have a kazillion things to do. I'm glad you're getting out though. Ya know, I could introduce you to some real cuties. Just say the word."

"I know, Monique. I know. Maybe one day I'll take you up on it." Bronze smiled.

"But not today, right? Just remember that I have two brothers; and those brothers come with friends. Sometimes when I stop by to see my parents, the house is crawlin' with fine, young tenderonis!" she added.

"I may be a late bloomer, Monique, but just because you started dating before you were out of diapers doesn't mean that everyone's like that!" They both laughed and headed back to the store.

That evening after-work traffic was heavy, but Angela Sommers was an experienced driver, and was accustomed to the congestion. Angela pulled up in front of Hubert's in her brand spanking new turquoise sports car. Her license plates proudly displayed her marital status SINGLE.

Angela was an administrative assistant with *Candor* magazine. She was a cinnamon-colored, sparkling woman with a slammin' boycut. Always the optimist, Angela was rarely without a boyfriend. Though she was the same age as Bronze, Angela had a maturity that Bronze attributed to her having three older sisters. Their friendship went back to junior high school. And even though they were the very best of friends, they both knew the importance of space. Sometimes weeks went by without the two touching base, but when they did, they'd make up for missed time. This evening would be one of those times.

Only two minutes went by before Bronze plopped

into Angela's passenger seat. She eagerly removed her feet from her sling-back pumps and slid them into a pair of comfortable low-heeled loafers as Angela whipped the car out of the mall parking lot.

"Rough day, huh?" Angela asked, keeping her eyes on the road.

"You got it. Can you drive faster before they send someone out to get me?" Bronze laughed. "Oh, don't let me forget to give you that new lipstick I told you about."

"What's it called?"

"Slick Cinnamon Stick."

"Oh, really now." She shook her head and grinned. "Who do you think names these shades, anyway?"

"Well, in this case either a cocky man or a horny woman," Bronze decided, laughing to herself. "Speaking of horny; girl I wouldn't mind a little cinnamon stick myself, right about now."

"How long has it been?"

"Put it like this. When I get on my knees at night, I'm tempted to say 'Lord, just send me a good man who can take care of business!'" Bronze clasped her hands and bowed her head in a mock prayer.

"Seriously, how long has it been since you got a good night's sleep, 'cause you know, if he does it right, you'll sleep all night!"

"What, about six, seven months?" Bronze shrugged.

"Whew! Girl, I think I'd be climbing the walls by now."

"Puhleez. I think I'm in hibernation," Bronze responded. "After a while, you forget it's even down there."

"Forget it's down there? The way mine purrs after a good tune-up? I don't think so."

"Honey, you'd be surprised." Bronze blew it off trying to minimize her situation, when the truth of the matter was she had spent many a night longing for some level of satisfaction.

They pulled up in front of a warmly lit storefront establishment, situated between a movie theater and a jewelry store. Thursday night at Ebony's was always packed. The after-work crowd loved to unwind amid the live music and good food. And for those who really wanted to get their groove on, there was a deejay and dance floor on the upper lever during the weekend.

As they entered, Angela immediately took note of how many men broke their necks to watch them both walk by. She was wearing the hell out of a black halter dress, which seemed to cling to her body for dear life. Her breasts sat high and perky, pushed together by a couple of clicks from an instant cleavage bra. Daily squats kept her derrière firm and round, and for Angela, it was a sin to miss a Pilate's session—which kept her muscles lean and sculpted.

"Can we turn heads or what?" she whispered to Bronze. Angela loved the effect she had on men, and it showed. Attention was just what she needed to put a little something extra in the sway of her walk. Like she always told Bronze, when a woman wears a catsuit, all the dogs will start barking.

"You're sure turning Dash's head."

Angela nodded to Dash the bartender. "It always pays to be in good with the bartender, especially when he makes the best apple martinis in town. But he needs to simmer a little longer before I let him take me out. See, Bronze, it's all about power, and I always plan to be the one in control. You gotta treat these jokers like they ain't nothin'; that's when they'll start sweatin' you hard and treating you like a queen."

Bronze, on the other hand, thought differently. She was a romantic. She hadn't had as much experience with men, and she didn't realize that they all played games.

They opted for a table up front, near the revolving stage centered in the restaurant. Thursday was jazz night, which meant that the saxophonists would have the spotlight. Bronze looked around. Everyone seemed to be having fun and laughter filled the air. Most of the men were dressed in suits, but the more relaxed ones removed their jackets and rolled up their sleeves, ready to take on the women as well as the upcoming weekend. None of them seemed worthy of Bronze's attention.

The waiter finally came to take their orders. Bronze chose the barbecued ribs and Angela decided on the jerk chicken. He returned shortly with their drinks: for Bronze an Irish cream on the rocks and an apple martini for Angela.

"So what are you going to do about this six-month dry spell, or hibernation as you put it? I mean, you act like you can't find anybody, and I know why; you're always sitting home at night. What's up with the men at work?"

Bronze instantly thought about Julian Mitchell. "Angela, it's not that serious . . . but," she paused and grinned. "I did meet someone. Remember the training I went to last month? Well, I met this gorgeous guy. . . ." Before Bronze could say anymore, Angela's cell vibrated on the table.

"Hold that thought; let me get this." Angela began to

talk in some magazine production lingo that Bronze didn't quite understand. Her thoughts drifted towards why she had even brought Julian up. He meant nothing to her, wasn't interested in her, and out and out embarrassed her in front of her peers. She hoped that by the time Angela ended her call, the conversation would be forgotten, realizing that the highlight of her love life was that some man ignored her for two days. How pathetic was that? Angela snapped her phone shut and picked right up where they'd left off.

"Okay, tell me about him so we can drool together." *Damn* Bronze thought. Just then the waiter arrived with their meals, set the plates before them and jetted off.

"He was indeed gorgeous, but he turned out to be the cockiest man I've ever met. That's pretty much the whole story," Bronze shrugged.

"So what was it about him that turned you on? He must have had something going for himself; you thought enough of him to bring him up. I mean, did he have big feet, good hair, what?"

"We all got together for drinks after class, and don't you know he completely ignored me?"

"And that was a turn on to you?" Angela laughed as she forked some rice into her mouth. Bronze told Angela about Julian—from his soulful eyes to his easy charm, then to his suggestive dancing that, quiet as it was kept, had her fantasizing all night long.

"And when Player stepped out on the dance floor with one girl on each arm, I was too through. I left all of them there."

"Good for you. To hell with him anyway with his blatant, arrogant self. But you know, dogs have their place."

"I know, in customs at the airport," Bronze said, and they both laughed.

"But I'll tell you what your problem is. You're too tense. Stop taking men so seriously. These guys aren't worth it. Don't you know male radars can detect when you're sweatin' 'em, and they'll run in the other direction? You gotta lighten up."

"Is that your secret?"

"That's it. I just told you, when you pay them no mind, they all get in line."

"Why do you always have to make something rhyme? You tryna get a rap deal or something? Well my name is Angie and I'm the best, all the deejays want to feel my. . . ."

"Shut up!" Angela laughed, tossing her napkin across the table at Bronze.

Angela ordered another drink while Bronze nursed her first one. The waiter returned with a tray full of scrumptious looking desserts. Although both women were as full as tics, they dared not pass up a slice of Ebony's famous sweet potato pecan pie. Bronze gave thought to Angela's theory of men handling, but knew she didn't have the sultry skill set to pull it off. She concluded that it just wasn't in her genes. And she certainly wanted more out of a relationship than a part-time non-committed lover. If there was really a God somewhere, The Right One would be along after while.

Bronze headed for the ladies' room as Angela signaled for the check. She returned, makeup freshened, and whispered to her friend, "You see that guy at the end of the bar? Now *that's* my type!"

"In the blue suit?"

"Uh-huh."

"Bronze, I know that guy."

"Get outta here." Bronze's eyes widened. She put her two hands together. "There is a God!"

"Yeah, that's Brandon Wilde. He works for *Candor* as a computer analyst. Come on; let me introduce you."

"No, wait," Bronze said, hesitating.

"You were just about to break out in a holy dance to praise the Lord, talking about 'there is a God,'" she mocked, "now you're scared to meet him. Girl, come on here." Angela grabbed Bronze's wrist and led the way to the bar. Angela feigned, surprised when Brandon noticed her.

"Angela, how are you?" Brandon asked.

"Brandon! I can't complain; I didn't know you hung out here." She rested her hand on his shoulder talking above the music and the enthusiastic crowd. "How do ya like the jazz tonight?"

"It's nice . . . very nice," he said giving Bronze a slow once over, indicating that the comment was more towards her than the music. She blushed.

Angela turned to introduce the two. "Bronze Sutton, Brandon Wilde."

He extended his hand.

"It's a pleasure." He smiled.

"Likewise." *Oh yeah, I could do something with this*, she thought.

"So what's up for the summer?" Brandon asked them.

"Not too much," Bronze started. "We were hoping to do some island hopping, but I just recently got promoted at work, so there's been a little change to my vacation plans."

"Yeah, and those car insurance payments are kickin' my butt," Angela added.

"That's right; you did just buy yourself a new cat-woman-mobile, didn't you?" Brandon nodded. "And you look good in it too! You need to take me for a spin in it soon; or you could just give me the keys and let me open it up for you on the highway . . . you know, to make sure she's running right," he chuckled.

In usual Bronze fashion, she made note of his eyes. She watched him as he talked with Angela. Brandon talked with his eyes. Very expressive. And she loved that mustache. Sexy. She took a quick glance at his hands. He wore only a square-faced gold watch. He was well groomed and she loved to see a man who knew how to take care of himself. No scraggly, ashy men for her. She made a quick assessment of his three G status. Well, he certainly looked and smelled good. She prayed for the opportunity to see if he would treat her good.

"We hafta get going," Angela said. "Maybe I'll see you tomorrow."

"Sure thing. And again, nice meeting you, Bronze."

"You too. Take care."

Chapter 4

Angela walked to her desk at *Candor,* grateful that the morning traffic had allowed for a few minutes to have her cappuccino and blueberry muffin, before she was officially on the magazine's time. As usual, she was the first one in.

Reading Paige Lawson's syndicated column on page ten of the *Daily Impressions* was also part of her morning routine. Not only did it keep her abreast of the country's celebrities, it also gave her ideas for future *Candor* articles.

While her ideas did not always gain acceptance into the upbeat African-American publication, they did gain her the respect of the editors who frequently held brainstorming sessions. So much so, that Angela was offered a position in the special projects department. Her boss, James Wilson, hated to lose her, but realized that the move would be a good one for the ambitious journalism major.

What was Paige Lawson saying this morning? The big story was the plans to have the Democratic National Convention in San Francisco the following

July. She quickly browsed over that story as something of greater interest caught her eye.

Which four-term Virginia Congressman may be calling it quits at the end of his term? Hint: He gives new meaning to the phrase 'doubling one's pleasure!'"

Angela made a mental note of that little tidbit for future reference. On second thought, she decided to tear out the column and place it in her folder; no sense in taking a chance and leaving something like this to memory. She checked her watch. The boss was due in exactly two minutes. Jagger Melrose walked in each morning at precisely 8:55. He was a stickler for punctuality and was determined to make the rest of the staff follow suit.

She skimmed through the rest of the newspaper and took the last bite of her muffin. *Five, four, three, two, one. Yup, here he comes.* She heard his irregular stride even before she saw him. Wounded in the Korean War, Melrose's left leg was a full three inches shorter than his right. At times Angela barely noticed his shortcoming, but when there was a deadline to meet, as there was this week, his pace became more pronounced and his breathing more accelerated. Sometimes Angela could almost see his densely populated nasal hairs being whipped around with each breath he took.

"Good morning, Mr. Melrose."

"Angela," he said, nodding.

She knew if she looked above his upper lip too long, she would burst out in an uncontrollable fit of laughter. As he passed her desk, she tried not to concentrate on the way he combed his hair over to conceal his bald spot, his elf-like, pointed ears or his gold-rimmed glasses.

The rest of the small staff trickled in just as Mr.

Melrose made his first cup of coffee. He didn't say a word, merely cleared his throat, making it known that he was keenly aware of the staff's regard for being on time, or the lack thereof. He glanced around the office taking note of the empty chairs of those who hadn't arrived yet, then went into his office closing the door behind him.

As the day progressed, the special projects department had its final meeting pertaining to the October issue of *Candor*. Once again Angela did not get a byline, but she refused to get discouraged. She told herself that it was just a matter of time before she made her mark in the literary world.

In fact, she relayed this sentiment to Brandon over lunch that afternoon. Angela had called Brandon, and the two agreed to do lunch in a nearby café, granting him his requested ride in her car. She didn't drive fast enough for Brandon's taste, having a sports car and all, but Angela refused to let a man call the shots in any area of her life if she could help it.

Angela went for a turkey sub, while after much contemplation, Brandon settled on a Philly cheese steak with sautéed onions. They decided to enjoy their meals outside in the Square and take in the sounds of summer—talented (and not so talented) street musicians, children's laughter, and the nostalgic melody from an ice cream truck.

"So, Brandon, how's life been treating you?"

"My work load is kinda heavy, but other than that, pretty good actually."

"I hear you and Terra from accounting are kickin' it," Angela dug for information.

"Nah. We're just friends." Brandon shook his head, quickly denying the allegation.

"But does *she* know that?"

"What do you mean by that? Of course she does."

"That's not what I heard. You men are good for pulling the 'just friends' card." She took a sip from her lemonade, raising her eyebrows at him demanding more of an explanation.

"You know how people like to gossip. This sandwich is some kinda good!" he commented through a mouthful of food, bringing his hand up under his chin to catch a would-be falling onion. "Anyway, does it matter?"

"Actually, it does. I wanted to hook you up with my girlfriend, but your plate's full.

"What girlfriend? The sistah that was at the club?" His mind raced back to meeting Bronze, remembering all of her features. Smooth skin, nice figure, quiet eyes, pleasant demeanor . . . all plusses. "Angela, do you know how long I've been waiting for someone like Bronze to come into my life?"

"Brandon, you don't even *know* her."

"Yeah, but first impressions last a long time. I can tell she's a gem, and I would treat her like a princess. Come on, Angela. Hook a brother up!"

"Tell you what. You clean up your act, and I'll see what I can do."

"Deal."

They spent the rest of the hour talking shop. Though it was only mid June, *Candor* was already in the early stages of planning its November issue. Naturally, the challenge was to arrive at fresh, new approaches for the holidays. As Angela well knew, this was the perfect time for putting on her creative thinking cap and shining in the eyes of her boss. Maybe she'd even get that long-awaited byline if she played her cards right. She said as much to Brandon.

"Angela, I think you must eat, sleep, and dream the almighty byline."

"Well, isn't that the name of the game around here? I mean, I can get a rush just thinking about it!"

"Tell me, professionally speaking, what would it take to flip your switch?"

"To be the editor-in-chief of my very own African-American women's magazine."

"So, eventually you want to start your own magazine?"

"You got it!" He nodded slowly, imagining her in a chief editor's role.

"Aren't you the ambitious one."

"Hey, there's nothing wrong with that, is there?"

Chapter 5

Stephanie climbed the stairs to her bedroom, anxious to kick off her heels and get out of her bone-colored silk suit. She and Bronze had gotten caught in traffic, making the ride home from Havenwood in Southern Ohio quite long. What was normally a six-hour drive turned into eight-and-a-half thanks to the state fair traffic. But what a splendid day it had been for her niece's wedding. There hadn't been a cloud in the sky and her brother Xavier was such a proud papa.

Going home to Havenwood always put Stephanie in a pensive mood. Sure, it was wonderful seeing her family, but the uneasiness came when she ran into nosy former neighbors and old classmates. How long would they keep her secret? On the other hand, how would Bronze react to the truth? Would it destroy her as it nearly did Stephanie twenty-six years ago? Would Bronze understand or would her love toward Stephanie turn to hate? Stephanie could not afford to take that chance, which was why she rarely went home. Yet and still, Stephanie resented being manipulated by the town folk's whims. And with that in mind, she and Bronze rushed back home.

They had arrived in Havenwood Friday evening to the loving arms of Stephanie's mother, who relished having her family together under one roof again. At seventy-five, Rose Sutton was by no means ready for a rocking chair. A glass of prune juice on the rocks every morning kept her in check.

Spry and alert, she got around without even the aid of a cane. "For old folks," she'd mumble to herself anytime her kids tried to get her to use one. And when Xavier, her youngest of three and only son, bought one for her one day, she didn't say a word. But two days later, he found it in her garden propping up her tomato plant. End of story.

Stephanie and Bronze had been the last to arrive. Though tired and a bit edgy from the long ride, both refused to succumb to their impulse to retire for the night. After all, wasn't family all about staying up until the wee hours of the night and reminiscing? Especially over Rose's famous—or rather infamous—zucchini cake. And who could deny Grandma? Bronze, the first grandchild, asked herself. It wasn't every day that three generations of Sutton folk were gathered under one roof.

Stephanie had glanced around at her family wishing all the while that her father could have been there too. But the Lord had called Stephan Sutton home almost thirty years ago. Her thoughts drifted back to her childhood. Stephanie still remembered how he would rush home from work at the railroad and get cleaned up just in time to play with her before tucking her in at night. She was the apple of his eye.

When Stephanie turned sixteen, the big question at school was who would take her to the junior prom. Her friends Dottie and Jean already had dates, but as usual, Stephanie could not find an escort. Not that she was unattractive or unpopular. Rather, when she brought someone home to meet her parents—or her father to be more exact—he'd purposely intimidate the young man.

"You picked him apart like he was a chicken bone," she remembered telling her father after another prospective date hit the road.

"You'll thank me one day," was all he said.

But Stephanie never did. In fact, none of the neighborhood boys could pass Stephan's inspection and word quickly spread that trying to court Stephanie was a waste of time and effort.

Eventually, the boys stopped calling altogether. This didn't faze Stephan in the least, but Stephanie paid the price for her father's over-protectiveness. After all, she was pretty and bright and felt that her high school years should be filled with fun. Her mother agreed and decided to intercede on her daughter's behalf. One night after the children had gone to bed, she had a talk with her husband. Eavesdropping, Stephanie still remembered the conversation as though it were only yesterday.

"Stephan," Rose had begun, "don't you think you've been too rough on Stephanie's suitors?"

"I will not have my daughter keeping company with someone who is beneath her."

"But they're not getting married for goodness sake. It's just a prom."

"Just a prom? That's how it all starts. Or have you forgotten?"

"Let me tell you something, Stephan. For sixteen

years I have stood by and watched you make a prima donna out of our daughter, but I said nothing because of the way my father ignored me for so many years. I even thought that your indulgence of her every whim could somehow make up for the treatment—or rather lack of treatment—I received from my father. But now I see that one extreme is no better than the other. Thank God she's not an only child or she'd probably be a spoiled brat. Can't you see that you're doing Stephanie more harm than good? For her sake I have to say something. Mark my words, Stephan. If you continue keeping Stephanie on that pedestal, one day it will come crashing down along with her. It's not right. You're setting her up for a big fall. What happens when she gets out in the real world and discovers that it's not the same as the rosy picture you've painted for her? And worse yet, what if you're not there to pick up the pieces? Then what?"

"Okay, Rose, I get your point," Stephan had admitted as he reached for the light switch and pulled the covers up around him.

Stephanie prayed especially hard that her father would allow her to attend the prom or to at least start dating like her other girlfriends. Unfortunately for her, Stephan was not ready to give up control and Stephanie remained relatively dateless throughout high school.

Two hours and one and a half zucchini cakes later, the Sutton clan decided to call it a night.

"Mama, Thelma and I are gonna leave now. We have to get ready for the final rehearsal and the dinner and make sure Vanessa gets all of her beauty sleep for the big day tomorrow," Xavier said.

"How is she, Uncle Xavier?" Bronze asked.

"A nervous wreck."

"Like any bride before her wedding," Aunt Thelma added.

Melissa and Raymond, Stephanie's niece and nephew, decided that it would be best for them to go home with their parents rather than hear their sister's mouth in the morning when she wondered where all her wedding party was.

Stephanie's sister Vy and her two girls were staying, which pleased both Stephanie and Bronze. It had been a long time since the three cousins were together, and their mothers had things to catch up on as well.

Stephanie and her sister slept in the second bedroom just off the kitchen while Bronze and her cousins Danielle and Alexis decided on the larger bedroom upstairs. Rose didn't know what time the rest of the household finally went to sleep, but when the living room clock struck three and she rolled over, the faint sounds of laughter could still be heard.

Morning came sooner than expected for the girls who stayed up until four talking about men, career choices, and *Sex in the City* episodes. They were awakened by the smell of their grandmother's golden pancakes and sausages, and it wasn't long before the trio joined the rest of the women at the kitchen table.

"Grandma," Danielle began, "I gotta hand it to ya, you can still burn some pots."

"Thank you, sweetheart. There's plenty. Eat up."

Stephanie looked around at her mother's kitchen. For as long as she could remember, it had been yellow and orange. Happy colors as Mama called them. And Mama was one of the happiest people Stephanie knew. "Honey," she would tell her children and grands, "when you get to be my age you realize that true happiness comes from within. If your search for happiness takes you outside of yourself, then you're on the wrong track. Don't ever forget that."

What was a beautiful morning turned into a glorious afternoon indeed for a summer wedding. The ceremony was held at the Mount Deliverance Church of God in Christ where the bride had been christened and baptized. It was a large, friendly church as Stephanie remembered, with its maple pews and red carpeting.

Stephanie watched as her brother and niece walked down the aisle, flashes popping all the while. That Vanessa was a beautiful bride was an understatement. The beaded and sequined gown only emphasized her petiteness, and her veil, once removed, revealed a flawless complexion.

As the bride and groom exchanged vows, Stephanie relived another time, another place. She reached over and gave her mother a hug. Stephanie looked at her daughter and smiled. In spite of everything else that may have gone wrong in her life, she had been blessed with a beautiful daughter. She remembered reading somewhere about the similarity in spelling between daughter and laughter and how a daughter should bring joy and laughter into her mother's life. She had gotten exactly what she had prayed for. This was no time for sadness. It was a time for celebration. Rose, who was seated between her daughter and granddaughter hugged them both to her chest. Her heart ached as well. They dried their eyes in time to see the bride and groom being pronounced man and wife.

The reception was held at the Apricot Room, en

vogue for weddings, parties, and the like. The banquet room opened to a lovely, outdoor gazebo, which showcased the well-manicured grounds. In all there were about 250 well wishers who gathered to be a part of Vanessa and Dave's grand day.

When the deejay played the electric slide, everyone, young and old, got up to dance. Stephanie was tickled watching the Greys, her mother's dear friends and neighbors. Mrs. Grey sported a daisy-covered straw hat and matching shoes. She and her husband had been married for over fifty years and were the life of the party. God bless them.

Later the cake was cut and the bouquet and garter thrown. Vanessa's sister Melissa caught the bouquet, at which point Xavier shook his head and yelled, "Give it back!" Everyone laughed. It was awfully expensive having daughters.

Stephanie and Bronze walked over to the newlyweds and offered their congratulations once again.

"Vanessa, dear, we're gonna get ready and hit the road." She put her hands around Vanessa's tiny waist.

"Okay, Aunt Steph. Thank you for sharing our wedding day with us. We know you don't come this way very often."

"Vanessa, I wouldn't have missed it for the world. Are you kidding?" She gave the couple a big bear hug. "And Dave, you be good to my niece."

"Absolutely."

Bronze and Vanessa promised each other that they'd do a better job of keeping in touch.

"Give me a hug, Bronze."

"Enjoy Paradise Island," Bronze said sincerely wishing them the best.

"Be happy," Stephanie said simply.

Chapter 6

The grand opening of Hubert's in the Middle Heights Mall went just as planned. The entire store was decorated with black, white, and red balloons—Lynn Hubert's favorite color combination.

What impressed Bronze the most was the pianist and saxophone player situated in the middle of the cosmetics department selling floor. Dressed in a black tuxedo, the pianist sat comfortably at a white baby grand piano while the sax player, who also wore a tux, stood by his side. They performed popular music from the seventies, eighties, and nineties, which Bronze thoroughly enjoyed. In fact, Bronze practically had a front-row seat as the piano was located just a few feet from the Velvet counter.

Melba Harte, the department manager, strolled through cosmetics from time to time to see how things were going and to check on sales. There were nine separate counters in all; each housed a cosmetic line manned by a full-time girl and a part-time assistant. It was Melba's job to visit each counter and get to know the sales associates. Although there had been a staff meeting earlier that morning followed by a department meeting, Melba still had a great deal to learn about her girls and their personalities.

Bronze couldn't remember the last time her feet had ached so. She ended up eating lunch in the employee lounge with her feet propped up. She spent the rest of the day behind the counter in her stocking feet. If Melba had something to say, so be it. Her dogs were barking.

To make matters worse, Bronze ended up staying past 9:30 when a customer couldn't make up her mind between two lipsticks. The final straw of her not-so-pleasant day came when Bronze rushed out of the store but ended up missing the last bus home that night. She fumbled in her purse for her cell phone, but as luck would have it, her battery needed recharging. It wasn't her night.

She walked to the phone booth in front of McDonald's to call a cab. Thank goodness she always kept a cab company's number in her wallet. The dispatcher told her they'd be there in about twenty minutes. So, she waited inside McDonald's. What else could she do? Bronze ordered a large chocolate milk shake and took a seat close to the door.

Out of the blue, someone gently tapped her on the shoulder. She turned around and gazed into a pair of the warmest brown eyes belonging to none other than Julian Mitchell.

"I thought that was you," he said simply. "How the hell are you?"

"Oh, hello," she said curtly, remembering him on the dance floor.

"Still mad at me, huh?"

"I don't know what you're talking about."

"Of course you do," he said, sitting down across from her. "You're mad because you require a lot of attention, and if memory serves me correctly, my hands were pretty full that night."

"Puhleez. Don't flatter yourself."

"Let me guess, Bronze. You're an only child. Am I right?"

Her response was a blank stare.

"I thought so. And see, I even remembered your name. That's how interested I was in you."

She shook her head and smiled. Men were a trip.

"What, you don't believe me? I bet I can tell you exactly what you wore those two days right down to your perfume." And that's precisely what he did.

Bronze had to laugh. She was impressed.

"Well it's about time you warmed up," he said, "but I bet you don't even remember my name, do you?"

"Of course I do. It's Jethro," she lied.

"Jethro? What do you think this is, *The Beverly Hillbillies*?"

"I was joking." She laughed.

"Can a brother get some respect?"

She laughed even harder. "Sorry about that, Julian."

"Oh, so you're playing games with me, huh?"

"No, but I just couldn't resist."

"You're lucky I'm such a forgiving guy." He noticed she'd glanced at her watch at least three times since he'd approached her. "So why do you keep checking your watch? In a hurry?"

"I missed the last bus home so I'm waiting for a cab."

"A cab? Let me do the honors."

"No, that's okay."

"But I insist."

"Are you sure?" she asked.

"Yeah. Let me just get my order and I'll take you home."

Walking alongside Julian, Bronze had forgotten just how tall he was, but she hadn't forgotten those eyes. They walked to his Accord, and she gave him directions to her house.

"Somehow I didn't think you lived here in Middle Heights," Bronze said.

"I don't. I live in Harvest Lake. I was on my way back from my cousin's crib when Mickey Dee's started calling my name. I feel like I haven't eaten all day," he said, grabbing a handful of fries from the bag.

He was a fast but careful driver, and she was home in no time. They exchanged numbers and agreed to keep in touch. Maybe Julian wasn't such a bad guy after all.

Angela called Bronze early one morning before she left for work. "Guess who has an extra ticket to tonight's Toni Braxton concert?"

"Not you."

"I certainly do. Wanna come?"

"Put it like this. Even if I had plans, which I don't, I'd cancel them. How'd I get so lucky?"

"Kevin got tickets for us, but his boss had to go out of town unexpectedly and offered to pay him double time if he'd hold down the fort tonight. And since he's seen her in concert about three times already, he handed over the tickets to me and told me to have a good time."

"And that we shall."

"I'll pick you up around seven. The concert starts at eight."

"Sounds great. See ya then."

At 8:37 Toni Braxton walked onstage, and the concert began. She sang songs from her latest CD, as well as some old favorites. For two solid hours she performed tunes to which all women in love could relate. When she performed *Un-break My Heart*, Bronze's thoughts went to Carlon. He had hurt her so badly. Before Bronze could dwell on the pain of what felt like salt on an open wound, Toni bandaged her back up by singing *Why Should I Care* and *He Wasn't Man Enough*. Before the concert ended, Bronze had been on an extended emotional rollercoaster, experiencing, love, hurt, pain, sorrow, laughter, freedom and empowerment. It was the best night she'd had in a long time.

"Now the fun begins," Angela said sarcastically as they exited the concert hall referring to the parking lot traffic, but they were back on the highway in a matter of minutes. They both had to work the next day, so she dropped Bronze off and promised to call her during the week.

Chapter 7

Bronze failed to hear her alarm clock go off, thus had to rush like a madwoman in order to get to work on time. While she stood waiting for her bus, black clouds threatened overhead. Luckily, the heavens didn't open up until after she got behind the counter, else she would have gotten completely drenched. The store was relatively empty except for a few customers who trickled in.

Bronze preferred to stay busy. At least that way the day sped by. But this way, the hours crept by at a snail's pace. Morning break seemed to take forever to arrive. When it finally did and she was able to poke her head outside for some air, it was still raining.

Later, while Bronze was engrossed in taking inventory of her existing stock, she looked up just in time to see a fine-looking brother headed her way. Julian. *Talk about putting the hot in a hot fudge sundae. Lord, have mercy.*

"How's it going?" he asked her.

"Slowly, very slowly."

He looked deeply into her eyes. "Some things are

good nice and slow." He paused. "What'd ya do, scare all the customers away?"

"It actually wasn't me more than it was that little thing called a thunderstorm."

"What's the world coming to when a woman lets a few raindrops come between her and a lipstick?"

"Don't they know they're messing with my commission?"

"Ain't that a bitch?" he asked, and they both laughed.

"Seriously though, what are you doing tonight after work?"

"Are you asking me out?"

"Maybe; are you accepting?" He lifted his hand to pick a small piece of Styrofoam from her hair and flicked it away.

"Could be."

"What time do you get off?"

"Six."

"Okay, I'll see you then."

Their first date. It was that simple. Bronze was still smiling to herself even after he left her counter.

Bronze kept checking her watch. Six o'clock couldn't come fast enough. But finally after what seemed like forever, it was time to go. She quickly ran a comb through her hair and freshened her makeup and perfume. When she walked out of the employee's entrance, Julian was there waiting for her in his black Honda.

"You smell delicious!" he said as she hopped in his car.

"Thank you, sir."

"What are you wearing?"

"Now, there are two things a lady never reveals, her age and her fragrance."

"What about her bra size?" he teased.

She gasped. "Julian, you're terrible."

"And you're what, a 34C?"

"Stop." she whispered. "You're embarrassing my twins!" She sheltered her bust with her folded arms.

"What, bigger? Smaller?"

"That's privileged information."

"Well, I plan on being in that inner circle. He winked.

"You're pretty sure of yourself, aren't you?"

"You'll see."

Bronze shook her head.

"So what do you feel like for dinner?" he asked. "Lady's choice."

"How about the Fickle Clam Bar?"

"That'll work."

By the time they arrived at the restaurant, it had stopped raining. A waitress seated them in a booth and barely gave them time to look over the menu. Bronze already knew what she wanted. Her mouth was watering for the stuffed shrimp, while Julian decided on a steak.

"So tell me, Bronze, who's the lucky man in your life?"

"There is none."

"You're kidding, right?"

"I wish I were."

"What's wrong with these men? Don't they recognize a good woman when they see one?"

"And how do you know I'm a good woman?" she asked. A slow smile spread across her face.

"Fishing for compliments, are we?"

"No. I just wanna see how good you are at reading me."

"Give me your hand," he said.

"What?"

"Give me your hand," he repeated.

She slid her right hand into his, enjoying the fit. He turned her hand over, exposing her palm.

"You see this line right here?" he asked, tracing a line just below her middle finger with his forefinger. "This means that you are a gentle soul at heart. But you're also a perfectionist. In your search for perfection," he added, "you're missing out on a lot. Let your hair down a little. Have some fun."

"What are you, a wannabe palm reader?" she asked as the waitress returned with their dinner.

"No, but I'm pretty perceptive. When's the last time someone jumped your bones?" He traced several small circles in her palm.

"Julian!" She snatched her hand away.

"Okay. I'm sorry. But girl, you gotta be overdue. I can feel it. And you know what they say. If you don't use it, it'll dry up on you."

Both speechless and embarrassed, she dug in her purse for nothing in particular. "Can we change the subject?"

"I'm sorry. Enough of this shock therapy. After all, this is our first date. Can we start over?"

"Please," she said simply. She'd barely gotten her fork in her mouth when Julian spoke again.

"How's your stuffed shrimp?"

"It's wonderful."

"Did I tell you I'm looking for another job?" he asked.

"Uh-un."

"Yeah. I've had it with retail. And between my rent, car payments, and child support, it's not enough."

"I didn't know you were a father."

"Yeah, I have a daughter. She and my ex-wife live in Atlanta." He paused for a moment as he looked out the window. "I miss my baby girl. Her mama won't even let me see her." There again was the familiar and painful prick of a father/daughter relationship gone awry. Bronze decided to sway the conversation back to its original point.

"So, have you been on any job interviews yet?"

"A few."

"Do you know what you wanna do?"

"Actually, I'm an artist, but Velvet keeps me from starving."

"You're kidding?"

"No. I'm an art major, and I freelance on the side. You should come by and see some of my work."

"I'm impressed, Julian."

"Have you ever had a portrait done?"

"No."

"Well, maybe one day you'll let me paint yours."

"Are you serious?" she asked.

"Absolutely. You'd be a perfect model. Look at you. You're more than just gorgeous; you're beautiful. An artist's dream. It would be my pleasure, Bronze."

"It would be my honor, Julian."

He gazed into her lovely, green eyes and smiled, draining his glass. She searched his eyes for a long moment then slowly returned his smile.

Chapter 8

Bronze and Angela rose early one morning and headed for the beach. The July sun teased Bronze's body as she shamelessly, in a bikini, permitted its sensuous rays to have their way. No other feeling could compare—except an orgasm, and she had nearly forgotten what one of those felt like.

She closed her eyes and allowed the sun to be her skillful, patient lover. So persistent. So intimate. Just the two of them. She shut out the rest of the world: the rowdy teenagers playing volleyball, the cute little toddler screaming as the waves tugged at her feet, forcing her to anxiously snatch at her mother's fingers. Bronze was addicted to the caressing her solar companion bestowed upon her. Its only desire seemed to be her pleasure, and she selfishly absorbed the attention. It was a very intense but brief affair. After all, summer did not last forever. Like most lovers, sooner or later it too would move on and she'd be left alone. So she enjoyed it while it lasted.

After a while, however, she could no longer stand the sun's intensity and was forced to her feet. A large, white cloud appeared, playing chaperone perhaps, and Bronze welcomed the chance to cool off. She found the water to be quite invigorating. Nevertheless, she was careful not to swim too far out past the shoreline.

Bronze marveled at how her girlfriend swam much farther out than she would ever dare. Angela was such a free spirit. She lived life to the fullest and had a real sense of adventure. Bronze envied that. She always played it safe. Sometimes too safe. Maybe Julian was right. Maybe it *was* time she let her hair down.

Bronze had to know. "Angela, have you ever gone skinny dipping?"

"*Me? Skinny dip?* Trust me, there's nothing skinny about my dip." She laughed. "Why do you ask?"

"Just curious."

"Hey, I have an idea. Let's check out that new Latin club tonight. The one on Palmetto Drive. What's it called?" Angela asked.

"La Vida Noche."

"Yeah, let's try it out."

"Angela." Bronze could think of a few other things she'd rather do than sit at a table with a drink amidst folks performing their homemade versions of the salsa or cha-cha. But then again, if she could find a handsome and suave Puerto Rican man to teach her a step or two, the night wouldn't be so bad.

"It'll be fun. Then we can stop by Ebony's afterwards if you like."

"Alright, alright. You talked me into it."

Bronze rummaged through her closet for something to wear. She decided on a short, reddish-orange strapless dress. The tangerine lipstick and nail polish were a perfect complement to her tanned skin. She chose a pair of strappy high heels to accentuate her feet, thankful that she had just had a manicure and pedicure the other day. In fact, just looking down and seeing her freshly pedicured toes in sandals was enough to give her a rush. It made her feel sexy. She let her hair fall around her shoulders, rather than pinning it up, envisioning her locks flying about while she spun in circle after circle.

She joined her mother who was busy fixing herself a snack in the kitchen.

"Boy, you are too hot to trot! Where are you on your way to?" Stephanie asked.

"Angela and I are going to that new Latin club, La Vida Noche," Bronze answered as Angela pulled up in the driveway.

Angela knocked on the door before entering.

"Come on in; it's open," Stephanie answered.

"Hi, Ms. Sutton."

"Hi, Angela. How's everything going?"

"Just fine; and for you?"

"Good. I'm glad you talked Bronze into going out tonight. Well, enjoy yourselves and drive safely."

"Yeah, we better get going, Bronze."

Half an hour later Bronze and Angela found themselves sitting at the bar of La Vida Noche. Hot Latin tunes filled the air and the two bartenders were real cuties. Bronze tried to keep up with the conversation between the couple on her left, but her Spanish interpretation skills were limited, and she soon gave up. Besides, they were talking a mile a minute. Angela asked Bronze to order her a rum and Coke while she went to the ladies' room.

"*Mami,* what ju want?" The bartender asked Bronze.

"Let me have a rum and Coke and a strawberry daiquiri."

"For ju, anything. Ju wearing contacts?" he wondered, referring to her eye color.

"No."

"No?"

"No," she repeated.

"Ju know, ju look like that actress. Ju know, Mees America."

"Vanessa Williams?"

"Aah, that's the one. *Mami,* where ju been all my life?"

"I don't know, but I'm here now." She grinned.

"Two drinks coming up." He winked.

Bronze watched as he prepared the drinks like a pro.

"These are on the house," he said. "Enjoy, *mi amor.*"

Angela returned ready to pay for her drink.

"These are freebies, compliments of the bartender," Bronze said.

Angela laughed and put her cash back into her purse. "I guess having you for a friend does have its privileges."

"Hey, and don't you forget it!" They both laughed.

By the time they finished their drinks, the club was packed. Thank goodness it was a smoke-free hotspot. Someone grabbed Bronze's waist from behind and kissed her gently on the cheek. Caught off guard, Bronze jumped.

"Care to tango, *mi amor?*" It was Julian.

Bronze was thrilled. "Well, you know, *papi,* it takes two to tango. Think you can handle it?"

"Try me," he said simply.

"Oh, Angela, this is Julian. Julian, Angela." She introduced them before Julian whisked her off to the dance floor.

Neither of them were pros, but they had a lot of fun doing the merengue or at least trying to. Bronze would first get dizzy from all the times Julian spun her around, then burning hot as he pulled her up against him. Instinctively, she raised her knee up to Julian's ribcage while he held fast to her thigh. His hand felt like fire, fire that quickly spread to all parts of her body. She felt his manhood rising up, and as their eyes locked momentarily, they sent him a clear message—she was loving every minute of what he was giving her. After three songs they decided to head back to their seats.

"Well, you guys certainly get an A for effort," Angela said. She nudged Bronze underneath the table.

"Thanks, but if I had had on my lucky socks, we would've made those other couples look catatonic," Julian said.

Bronze's temperature was so high, she could barely speak. Not to mention Julian had seriously turned on the flex appeal.

"Bronze didn't need lucky socks though; she was burning up the floor! And she already has that Latin-looking flavor going on anyway." He bit his bottom lip as he looked at Bronze. "Girl, you look so fly, you give new meaning to the phrase Spanish fly."

"Julian, if that's not a player line, I don't know what is." Angela shook her head, laughing.

"Now why is it that every time a man expresses his appreciation of a beautiful woman, he has to be a player? Can't a man be honest without being labeled?" Julian asked.

"He certainly can, but don't forget I've already seen you in action and the proof is the truth," Bronze added, though pleased that she didn't have to share her dance with Julian with some skank.

"Can't a brother have a little fun?"

"Define fun," Bronze said; her own ideas swam in her head.

"I wish to plead the fifth on the grounds that I might incriminate myself."

"I think that's the smartest thing you've said all night," Bronze pointed out.

Chapter 9

The end of summer was drawing near. Normally, this would be a time of melancholy and introspection for Bronze, but not this year. For the first time in quite a while Bronze was not saddened. In fact, she would usher in the fall with as much enthusiasm as she would normally reserve for the onset of her favorite season. The reason could be summed up in two words, Julian Mitchell. The more she saw him, the more she wanted to see him. She found him so damn sexy. She could really fall for him. *Slow down, we're just friends*, a small voice inside told her.

One night before he picked her up to see a movie, she asked her mother for her opinion of him.

"Well," Stephanie began, "I've only met him a couple of times, but he seems nice enough." Bronze could sense that her mother wanted to say more, but she had left it at that.

They saw Nia Long's new flick at the multiplex. Nia played a waitress in love with twins, both played by Morris Chestnut. One was a pro-football star, the other a school teacher. After the movie Bronze and Julian stopped by TGIF's for a quick bite to eat. She wasn't much for conversation. While she enjoyed the movie, what her mother *didn't* say ate away at her all night. She scolded herself for being so hung on her mother's approval, not understanding why it was so important to her. Bronze was a grown woman, able to make her own decisions, choices and assessments. So what if her mother didn't like him. She liked him, and the Three Gs were in effect, so who cared what Stephanie felt. Julian brought her attention back to the forefront.

"Talk about fantasy. Stuff like that only happens in the movies. How many women do you know would pass up a chance to marry a professional athlete to marry a teacher? This should've been a comedy."

"Not every woman's a gold digger, Julian."

"But, Bronze, she was a freakin' waitress."

"And your point?"

"Obviously, her dogs weren't barking loud enough. A few more years and I guarantee you she'd wish she had gone pro."

"Did you ever stop and think that maybe, just maybe, she followed her heart and married for love?"

"And give up the vacations, the cars, the beautiful house, the—"

"Like Luther Vandross said, 'A house is not a home.' "

"But that's just a song, Bronze. A song. So, in other words, you're telling me that you would've done the same thing?"

"Yes, if I loved the teacher, I would have."

"Aaaw shit."

"What's the famous line from Hamlet?"

"What? To be or not to be?"

"No; to thine own self be true!"

* * *

The next few weeks, Bronze and Julian monopolized all of each other's free time. They went to movies, clubs, museums, art exhibits, all kinds of places together. They even started playing tennis and joined a gym.

After a while, they seemed inseparable. She had just gotten in from working late one rainy Saturday night when her phone rang. It was Angela.

"Hey, girl, long time no see. What's up?"

"I'm taking a much-needed break tonight. Staying in." Bronze pulled a pair of satin pajamas out of the drawer in preparation for bed.

"What? No Julian?"

"Oh, come on. We're not *that* bad."

"Are you kidding? Lately, I feel like I need an appointment just to talk to you!"

"Stop." She laughed as she plopped on her bed.

"I'm serious. Did you give him any yet?"

"No. We're just friends."

"Puhleez."

"No, really."

"Bronze, you are in serious need of a reality check. One of these days he's gonna charm you right out of your panties, and you'll love it."

"Whatever."

"Okay, we'll see. Anyway, keep me posted. Let's do brunch tomorrow."

"Sound's good. At the Square?"

"Perfect."

"Alright, girl. Later."

Bronze ran herself a nice hot bubble bath. After the day she'd had at Hubert's, she felt like she could soak for hours. The water was so soothing she had almost dozed off. Then the doggone phone rang again. It was Julian.

"Whatcha doing?"

"I'm in the tub," she said in her most mellow voice.

"Ooh, sounds inviting. Mmmm," he moaned.

"What's new?"

"I need to see you, Bronze. Now."

"Julian, it's pouring rain out there."

"Be ready in half an hour or I'm joining you in the tub!"

Damn. Her bubble bath went down the drain as she put on a pair of jeans and a white T-shirt. True to his word, Julian picked her up exactly thirty minutes later.

"Where are we going?" she asked.

"Nowhere . . . anywhere." He drove a few miles in silence and parked by the lake. "I had to see you, Bronze. There was no way in hell I was gonna let a few raindrops stop me from seeing you tonight." He turned to gaze in her eyes. "And to think I didn't even like you when I first met you, Miss Stuck-up."

"You didn't like me? I couldn't stand you, Mr. Full of Yourself. And look at us now."

"Who would've thunk it?"

"Who would've thunk it?" she agreed, laughing softly.

Gazing into her eyes, Julian eased forward until their lips were barely apart. Finally, they kissed. Bronze had waited so long for his touch. From the moment she looked into his eyes and was reminded of hot cocoa, she knew she needed him the way a chocoholic craved a candy bar. And the more time they spent together, the stronger the urge had become.

She opened her mouth, and his tongue found hers, eagerly, hungrily. *Oh, God, he feels so good.* She wanted so much more of him. Slowly, he reached for her breast, and she let out a soft moan. She kissed him with all the longing of a woman who had not had sex in nine months, and he gave it right back to her, stroke for stroke. Bronze loved the feel of Julian's warm hands on her back. He brought his hands from her back to her front and slid them underneath her bra, finding her bare breasts. It had been so long since Bronze had felt a man's touch, and she was quickly learning to appreciate Julian's. He lifted her blouse and lowered his head to take pleasure in her nipples. Bronze gasped as her head tilted backwards and met the head rest.

If it weren't for the sudden loud barking of a stray dog, they may have climbed into the back seat like a couple of teenagers. The noise, however, zapped them back to the reality of their surroundings.

"Whew!" they both said at the same time as they laughed and settled back into their seats.

"I guess you're no ice princess after all," he said.

"Never said I was," she responded as she adjusted her clothes.

"So how the hell are ya?"

"Hot," she said, laughing.

"You know, I have a remedy for that." He rubbed the nape of her neck.

"Do you now?" She looked at him slyly.

"Absolutely."

"Is it a sure cure?"

"No doubt?"

"I hope it's a suppository."

"Ooh, you've got game! You have the face of an angel and the mind of a devil. I knew you'd be phat. I could see it in your eyes, and you know the eyes never lie."

Chapter 10

Labor Day came and went, and Stephanie settled into the new school year amid the changing colors of the autumn leaves. Teaching kindergarten was such a joy, and she prayed each day for the patience and guidance necessary to facilitate her students' learning. For her, it was more than just a j-o-b, it was an awesome responsibility. She was shaping little minds, and thus, the future as well. She held back a smile as one little boy called her Miss Sumptin. Naturally, it was contagious, and by the end of the day, half her class was calling her Miss Sumptin too.

When she returned home, her daughter already had dinner on the table.

"Wow! To what do I owe this pleasure?" Stephanie asked.

"You deserve a break," Bronze said simply.

"Well, it smells delicious. I'm famished. What's up?" She knew her daughter.

"I know I asked you this already, but what do you think of Julian? The truth this time, Ma."

"He seems okay, and he's definitely a charmer."

Stephanie thought for a moment, wanting to choose her words wisely. "Bronze, I don't know how to put this so I'm just going to come right out and say it. Is Julian gay?"

"Is he what?" Bronze nearly choked on her salad. "Where did that come from?"

"He reminds me of an old college friend of mine."

"No, he's not gay! He's as straight as an arrow. How could you even think that?"

"Relax, it was only a question; just a vibe I guess. I could be wrong. Just be careful. I don't want to see you hurt."

"Don't worry about me. I'm a big girl."

That night as Stephanie lay in bed, her mind drifted back to her college days. She remembered a smooth, charming, handsome man who turned out to be bisexual. His fiancée was totally devastated when she discovered his secret. She hadn't seen the signs; consequently, she paid dearly for it. Her life was forever changed. If only she had known, it would have saved her much heartache. Stephanie prayed that she was wrong about Julian. She wasn't sure if Bronze could handle it if she wasn't.

Bronze and Julian met at Ebony's after work one evening for dinner and drinks. Unable to contain himself, Julian blurted out the good news.

"I got the job, Bronze. You're looking at Millard Publishing's new cover artist!"

"Congratulations!" They embraced in a tight hug that ran both their thermometers up a few degrees.

Bronze was the first to pull away, not wanting to start any trouble. "Dinner's on me," she smiled.

"I can't let you do that."

"Sure you can." Julian started to protest a second time, but Bronze threw her hand up to silence him. "I insist." Julian waved his napkin in the air as a sign of surrender. "So when do you start?" she asked.

"I gave the store two weeks notice, and then it's bye-bye Velvet, hello Millard Publishing!" The excitement was evident in his voice.

"That's wonderful."

"I'm throwing a party Saturday night at my place, and I want you to come."

"I'd love to. Is there anything you want me to bring?" she asked.

"Just your normally gorgeous self." She blushed.

"I try."

"You're so modest," he commented.

"That's not what you thought when we first met."

"You must have been PMS-ing that day."

"Maybe."

"Let's dance," Julian said as the deejay played some Gerald Levert. Bronze sang in Julian's ear as they flowed to the music. "Are you really ready, baby?"

She looked him straight in the eye without blinking, then nodded slowly.

Chapter II

Bronze and Angela met to go shopping for an outfit for Julian's party.

"I'm not just looking for *a* dress, I'm looking for *the* dress," Bronze said.

"Sounds like you plan on doing the do that night."

"Repeatedly." She laughed. "So, I need a dress that'll show off all my assets."

They drove out to the mall but after two hours, had no luck there.

"Let's try that little boutique across town by the library. If we hurry, we can catch them before they close," Angela suggested, putting the pedal to the metal.

The minute they got there, Bronze spotted her outfit. It was a sleeveless, short, supple black leather dress. She tried it on, and it fit like a glove.

"Perfect," Angela said as Bronze modeled it for her. "I don't know how long it'll take you to get into it, but I know it'll only take a hot minute for him to get you out of it."

"That's exactly what I want."

* * *

Bronze was having the time of her life Saturday night at Julian's party. The look on his face when she took off her coat, revealing the little black dress, made it worth every penny she paid for it. The drinks were flowing, the food was delicious, and the music was jamming. She met a lot of his friends, and they treated her like she was The One. Apparently, Julian had told them all about her.

"So, you're the girl who's been keeping our boy from us," Julian's buddy, Aramis York, said. He was a well-built brother with a freshly shaved head.

"Can't say I blame him though." Matt Simpson winked. He and his wife, Melanie, had known Julian since childhood. Melanie was over at the bar refilling her drink.

Matt was the deejay for the night. When he played, *You Know That I Love You* by Donell Jones, Julian grabbed Bronze's hand and pulled her up to dance.

"You know you're wearing the hell out of that dress," he whispered in her ear.

"Let's see how long it takes you to get me out of it after the party," she whispered back.

"You wouldn't tease a brother, would you? Are you saying what I think you're saying?"

"What exactly do you think I'm saying, Mr. Mitchell?" She felt his third leg along her thigh.

"That you're gonna give me some tonight, Miss Sutton."

"Then, I'd say you're absolutely right."

At that point, Bronze stepped out on the terrace for some air leaving Julian to pull himself together.

The air felt good against her bare arms. She looked

up at the mid September sky and wondered what the night had in store for her—or rather, for them. Whatever it was, Lord only knew how long they had both waited for it, wanted it. Tonight would be their night.

Julian slid up behind her and wrapped his arms around her waist, kissing her on the nape of her neck.

"You don't know how long I've been looking forward to this," he said.

"Yes, I do."

"How long?"

"Just as long as I have." She subtly pushed her behind up against him, allowing him a small sample of what she planned to put on him later.

"Mmm . . . back that thang up, girl. You sure you're not gonna change your mind?" he asked.

"I'm positive," Bronze said matter-of-factly as they headed back inside.

She went to the bathroom to freshen up her makeup. When she returned to the party, she glanced around for Julian, but he was no where to be found. Not wanting to look conspicuously insecure and immature, Bronze found Melanie in the kitchen cutting cake and struck up a conversation.

Melanie talked about everything from her job, to her kids, to her cake recipes. She had kept Bronze sufficiently distracted and entertained until Julian magically appeared an hour later.

"Where you been, baby" Bronze whispered as she nestled into his arms. "I missed you."

"Oh, uh," he pecked her lips quickly. "Me and my boy had to run out and get some more ice for the cooler." He bent to whisper in Bronze's ear. "I'ma save some of that ice for later and see if I can't cool you off a little bit." Just his words sent a jolt through her spine.

"Forget later; meet me in the bedroom in five minutes!" She slid her hand from around his waist to the front of his pants and gave a little squeeze.

"You know what to do with that thang, girl?" he moaned in her ear.

"Come find out." At that she spun away from him and switched upstairs, not caring who may have been watching.

Julian poured the ice in the cooler and immediately went upstairs where Bronze was waiting for him in his bedroom. Upon his entrance he closed the door and pulled her to him, sliding his hands up her dress all the while. He was delighted when his hands discovered bare skin and the tiny string of a thong. In a matter of seconds, he pulled the dress above her head and dropped to his knees. Bronze let out a cry as he settled his mouth over the small triangle of fabric that covered the prize he wanted. She placed her hands on his head for both guidance and balance, then lifted her leg and wrapped it around his shoulder, opening up to him. Julian wasted no time in using his tongue to take her to a place she had not been in forever, even right through her panties. As she came, she melted onto his bedroom floor, begging him to take her right there, but he held back.

"Just stay right there baby. I'll be right back."

"Julian, don't leave me like this," she moaned and pleaded. Her back arched pushing her breasts forward to meet his lips. He teased each nipple alternately for the next few minutes, causing her to have an erotic conniption.

"I promise; I'll make it worth your wait . . . let me get these people outta here so you can scream as much as you want." At that he slid away, leaving her hungry and wanting, but assured that she would sleep well that night.

It took another forty-five minutes for the last coat to disappear from the guest room bed, which was torture for Bronze; she was ready for the fun to begin. She pressed her ear to the door for a few seconds, and after hearing nothing, she took her bra off, but kept on her wet thong and stilettos, and waltzed out of Julian's bedroom and down the stairs to find him. Bronze headed for the kitchen where she could hear water running.

"Can't you do that later," she called rounding the corner, certain that the twins would make him stop dead in his tracks.

Her voice startled him and he spun around suddenly, but not before he could adjust his open pants. Aramis scrambled to rise off the floor, but it was too late.

Bronze was going to be sick. Not caring that she was just an inch of fabric away from being naked, Bronze stood for a full five seconds in shock and disbelief, before she whirled around and bolted up the stairs. She ran back into the bedroom with Julian on her heels. She slammed and locked his bedroom door before he could get inside.

"Bronze, open the door," he yelled, his fist pounding against the wood. Bronze snatched up her dress and fought frantically to get in it. When she opened the door, Julian grabbed her in an attempt to stop her from leaving.

"Get off me!" She pushed him away.

"Wait a minute, Bronze. It's not what you think. Just listen to me."

"What, you think I'm stupid? I know what I saw. Stay away from me, Julian."

"Let's talk," he pleaded.

"Talk? There's nothing to talk about. I never want to see you again." Bronze snatched up her coat and left.

She must have done close to seventy miles per hour all the way home in her mother's car, before she fell completely apart in the driveway. She was so ashamed. Why hadn't she listened to her mother?

The next couple of weeks were excruciating for Bronze. She could barely keep anything on her stomach, and she was always in tears. Julian left messages on her cell phone around the clock. When he did get through, she would hang up without giving him a chance to charm himself back into her life. At work, she would go into the stockroom and cry. A couple of times she had to run to the ladies' room, the bile rising up in her throat, her face flushed with shame. Once, when Deandra asked her if she'd been crying, she blamed her red eyes on allergies.

When it got to a point where she could no longer keep her feelings bottled up inside, she confided in her mother. Stephanie never once said, I told you so. She took her daughter in her arms and rocked her gently. When Bronze hurt, Stephanie hurt. They cried together.

Finally, Stephanie wiped her daughter's tears away and handed Bronze a tissue to blow her nose.

"Now, look at me," Stephanie said, but Bronze held her head down in shame. She took her daughter's face in her hands until their eyes met. "You don't have anything to be ashamed of," Stephanie said softly. "You hold your head up high. That's what your grandfather used to tell me, and that's what I'm telling you. You did nothing wrong, Bronze. You simply followed your heart. But this, too, shall pass. Trust me."

Promise? Bronze wanted to ask.

As if reading her mind, Stephanie added, "I promise."

Eventually, Bronze called Angela to fill her in on the latest.

"Damn, I should've figured him out," Angela said. "I'm usually pretty good at it."

"It's not your fault. It was my mistake. I guess I didn't do my homework," Bronze said with regret.

"Well, think of it this way. At least he didn't get the kitty. That really would've been a mess."

"I know you're right, but I'm still hurt."

"And you have every right to be. He wasn't honest with you. Hey, I know. Let's get our toes done; my treat." Bronze knew she wouldn't be the best company for anyone given her mood.

"Nah, I'm not really up to it, but I'll take a rain check."

Little by little, Bronze's pain began to subside. She began working late hours and overtime to keep herself busy. It got to the point where all she did was work, eat, and sleep, keeping her social life non-existent. Not quite ready to get back in the game and put her heart on the line again, she shied away from any advances from the male species.

When she felt enough time had elapsed, Angela stepped in. "Bronze, you can't continue avoiding men altogether! It's like riding a horse. If you get thrown off one, you gotta get back up, dust yourself off, and try it again. The longer you wait, the harder it'll be. Trust me. Let's say we go to Ebony's tonight."

"Maybe some other time." Getting back on the horse was the absolute last thing on Bronze's agenda.

"Look, I'll bet you a trip to the nail salon that you'll have a good time. Who knows? You might even meet someone tonight."

"Angela, I don't care to meet anyone." Bronze yawned and stretched out on her bed. She grabbed the remote from her nightstand and turned on her 19" television.

"So you're just going to sit around and dry up, never to be seen or heard from again?" Angela picked up on the sound of the TV in the background. "This is the rest of your life, huh? Work and reruns." Bronze, sensing that Angela's coercing would only come to an end if she hung up on her, finally yielded.

"All right. You talked me into it; as long as I'm home early. I have to work tomorrow."

"No problem."

An hour later, Bronze and Angela were among Ebony's Saturday night crowd enjoying the pulsating beat of the house music. It couldn't compare to Thursday night's jazz, but it wasn't bad. Bronze had to admit, it felt pretty good to be out again.

"Angela, Bronze, nice to see you again. Can I join you?"

"Sure." Angela slid over towards the wall making room in the booth for Brandon. "Bronze, you remember Brandon?" Angela asked.

"Of course." A slight smile unintentionally appeared on Bronze's face, which Brandon quickly took note of.

"Do you come here often?" he asked Bronze.

"Mostly on Thursdays. How about you?"

"Yeah, I like the jazz scene myself." He signaled for the waiter who appeared momentarily to take their orders. The waiter returned with Angela's Apple Martini, Bronze's White Russian, and Brandon's Screwdriver. Brandon insisted on paying for the drinks.

Angela accidentally spilled her drink on her sweater. She excused herself and headed for the ladies' room. Neither Brandon nor Bronze missed her company. She fought against it, but she was attracted to Brandon. They were in their own little world, and their body language spoke volumes. Bronze especially liked his hearty laugh and the way he gently touched her arm to make a point.

When Bronze got home that night, she took a long, hot shower, letting the water concentrate on her back and chest. Now more than ever she was reminded of her 3-G standard. Well, he looked and smelled good, but would Brandon treat her good? Only time would tell.

Chapter 12

From the moment Bronze and Brandon hung out at Ebony's that night, their appetite for each other had been whet. But since both were on the rebound, they were understandably cautious. In fact, they included Angela on their first three dates, and it was only after she insisted that she wouldn't spend another evening baby-sitting her friends that Bronze and Brandon decided to go it alone.

For their first solo venture they opted for a sunset jazz cruise. It rained all morning long, and Bronze was worried about spending a soggy night at the lake that evening. Especially, since it was sneezin' season. Luckily, the rain stopped around noon, though the sun never did make an appearance that day.

One of the perks of working in cosmetics was the many fragrances available at her fingertips. And she had heard from Angela that Brandon's favorite perfume was Forever. She dabbed a hint behind each ear and on a few choice pulse points before they met that evening.

Each time they went out she had been impeccably

dressed and groomed. Not tonight. Her hair flopped from the weather, and it was that time of the month. Needless to say, Bronze was not in the best of moods. She even thought about calling Brandon and canceling. But when he picked her up from work, she was glad that she hadn't broken their date, regardless of her appearance, her cycle or her mood.

They pulled up at the pier and looked for parking. Brandon and Bronze had just enough time to find a spot and board the boat before it set sail.

They ordered drinks and appetizers before the band began performing. Brandon looked at Bronze. Bronze looked up and matched his stare, the intensity forcing her hand to her hair in a nervous gesture. Brandon, in turn, took his hand and began stroking her hair, his eyes never leaving hers. He dropped his hand to her jaw and gently caressed her chin; all while bringing her face closer to his. Their lips met and they kissed. Bronze was the first to pull away.

They sat through two hours of live jazz-fusion, and though the music was outstanding, neither of them really paid it much attention. Both of them were engrossed in thoughts of each other and barely noticed that their food grew cold.

They went out on the deck and enjoyed the cool breeze off the water. The night air was damp, and Bronze shivered.

"Chilly?" Brandon asked.

"Yes," she said simply. He removed his jacket and placed it around her shoulders.

"Better?"

"Much," she admitted. The third G seemed to be in place, but there was more fact-finding to be done.

The sounds of the band floated to the outer deck, enhancing the moment. "Let's dance," he said, gently pulling her towards him.

The band played a slow, sultry tune, and Brandon and Bronze flowed into each other's arms. They danced in silence for a few moments, not trusting their voices to speak, but allowing their bodies to do the talking for them.

Finally, Brandon cleared his throat. "When can I see you again?"

"When do you want to see me again?" she asked coyly.

"Are you busy tomorrow night?"

"I am now," she answered.

The song ended, and Bronze and Brandon returned to their table. He reached for her hand and gently squeezed it. She searched his eyes wondering if she was ready for him.

Chapter 13

Stephanie woke up, showered, and put on a pot of vanilla latte. She heard the newspaper hit her front door, and before long she was reading Paige Lawson's column.

My sources tell me that Congressman Prescott has been spotted once again—or should I say thrice again—at Club Desire with more than just a drink in his hand. Seems he can't get enough of that Indianapolis hotspot. For those of you not in the know, Club Desire caters to gay men. Anyway, the Congressman had to be swiftly removed from the premises when he propositioned the wrong guy, and the man's, shall we say boy toy, told him not only where to go, but the fastest way to get there! Don't you just love friendly politicians? And speaking of friendly, writer Paula Reese's sizzling new novel will be brought to the big screen by Canon Pictures. PR agreed to the deal with the mega movie studio when they signed Isaac Cunningham as the director. Production will begin in early spring. As you may recall IC and PR were old college chums, and even though they're two thousand miles away, they're closer than ever. Gee, if only those old dormitory walls could talk.

Stephanie wasn't the only one reading Paige Lawson's column that morning. Angela sat at her desk at *Candor* magazine sipping cappuccino when she was hit with the perfect idea—an article on bisexuality in the African-American community. Both the piece on Prescott and Bronze's experience with Julian had set her wheels in motion. She decided to run it by her boss at their weekly special projects brainstorming meeting later that morning.

Three stories up, Brandon sat at his desk wrestling with the idea of calling his old flame Capricia Moore. From the moment he heard her familiar voice on his voice mail two days ago asking for a return call, the memories had crept back into his consciousness.

It hadn't been easy getting over her after their five-year relationship. Hell, he even shared his apartment with her, not just his body, breaking a cardinal male rule. But she wanted her independence and the freedom to date others, claiming she felt stifled. He blamed a lot of their problems on her so-called girlfriends. One day while he was at work she packed up her belongings and left. Her departure had not been the culmination of an explosive argument or threatening scene. Maybe that's why he was totally caught off guard.

When he arrived home that evening there were no traces of her in his apartment, except for the Dear John letter on his pillow. He hadn't wanted to pick it up, let alone read it, but he had to face reality.

Brandon,

You're a sweetheart, but it's time for me to move on. I've already told you that I want to see other people and because I respect you enough not to cheat on you, I feel this is best. Although you're wonderful, I've got to know that I'm not missing out on my soul mate.

Always Love,

Capricia ♥

He felt as though he had had the wind knocked out of him. It was over. They were through.

That was a year ago. Occasionally, they'd bump into each other at the mall, and once Brandon ran into Capricia at an Anita Baker concert. They both loved the singer. But other than that, they were no longer a part of each other's lives, not even as much as a phone call had transpired between them. In fact, the last thing Brandon heard, Capricia had moved to Atlanta.

He decided to return her call. After all, he was over her. Capricia had no control over his emotions. She was completely out of his system. Yet, with mixed emotions, he dialed her number.

"Hello, stranger. I didn't think you were going to call me," Capricia admitted.

"Why wouldn't I call?" Brandon asked, trying to keep it light. "We're old friends."

"Then let's get together and talk about old times," Capricia suggested. "They weren't all bad, you know." Brandon attempted to control the slight rise he felt in his pants stimulated by Capricia's mellow and sensuous voice. He remembered her cooing and moaning softly in his ear during one of their many lovemaking sessions. He cleared his throat, trying to redirect his thoughts.

"Are you in town? I heard that you'd moved to the A-T-L."

"I did. I had to come take care of some business. I'm here for a few more days . . . and nights." She knew Brandon would catch her drift.

Aw, what the hell, he thought before speaking. "Well, how's lunch tomorrow sound?" Brandon figured lunch had to be safer than dinner.

"Sounds great. I'll meet you at The End Zone at one."

"See you then, Capricia," Brandon said. As he stretched back in his chair, he breathed a sigh of relief. Their conversation hadn't been so difficult.

Brandon's thoughts quickly switched to Bronze. He couldn't remember the last time he had waited so long to be with a woman or had wanted a woman so much. Hell, he had slept with Capricia on their second date, but he knew from the moment he met Bronze that she would be different, but sleeping alone had never appealed to him. Here it was a month into their relationship, and they were still playing footsy. And after a while, cold showers just didn't work, which was why he always kept a female stashed away for emergencies. It was purely physical. No expectations. He would set the woman straight from jump street. She'd know there was no future for them. Just a helluva lot of phenomenal banging. Bronze, on the other hand, was a challenge. And he was definitely up to the challenge. But in the meantime, he needed to relieve a little tension.

Chapter 14

Stephanie returned home from a day filled with busy five-year-olds. She loved her kindergarten children, all fifteen of them. Sometimes she wished that she had had more of her own. Not so much for her sake but for Bronze's. As a child Bronze had always wanted siblings, but once she realized that none were coming, she adjusted.

In fact, even now she sometimes told Stephanie, "You're *my* mother, and I don't have to share you with *anybody*! You're *all* mine." She seemed to enjoy saying that.

Stephanie remembered when a five-year-old Bronze climbed into her lap and asked about her father, and how it brought uncontrollable tears to her eyes. Life could be so unfair. Why must children suffer for their parents' decisions? She'd cried so much, it wasn't long before Bronze wailed right along with her, although she never understood her mother's pain.

"Don't cry, Mommy." She used her small hands to smear away Stephanie's tears. "I won't ask you about

Daddy again." Sobbing and gasping, Bronze wrapped her pudgy little arms around her mother's neck.

"I'm afraid we're all we've got, kiddo," she told her daughter.

Later that evening as Stephanie led Bronze into her bedtime prayers, she asked God to give her daddy a kiss for her and to tell him that she and her mommy loved him. Stephanie cried all night.

Bronze's voice jolted Stephanie back to the present. "I'm home."

"In the kitchen, hon."

"Ma, I just found the perfect apartment over on Holloman Way by the junior high. Two bedrooms and a living room, and get this, a cozy little window seat like I've always wanted. Ma, you gotta see it. I could really do a lot with it, and the rooms aren't puny either. Oh, and there's plenty of closet space too. I'm telling you, it's me."

"Sounds good." Stephanie dropped a few pieces of floured chicken into a pan of sizzling oil, then washed her hands. "Can you handle the rent?" She peeked into the oven at her macaroni and cheese.

"Ma, I've saved up more than enough money for the deposit and first month's rent, seeing how I've been working like a mad woman here lately. And the rent is really affordable. I may have to cut back on a few of my shopping sprees, though."

"Did you leave a deposit?"

"No. I wanted you to have a look at it first. She looked at Stephanie, once again seeking her mother's approval. "Feel like taking a ride?"

"Do I have a choice?" she laughed. "You'll have to wait until this chicken finishes though." Forty minutes later Bronze drove Stephanie the short distance to Holloman Way, nearly running a red light in her haste to reach the brick building situated on a well-manicured lawn adorned with two big mimosa trees.

"And another thing, Ma, the bus to the mall stops right around the corner, and there's a Laundromat down the street."

It only took Bronze a minute to get the keys to the third-floor apartment from the rental office. She climbed the stairs two at a time while Stephanie trailed behind wishing for an elevator, but also feeling the third floor offered a little security against thieves.

"Well, this is it, Ma," Bronze announced as she opened the door to what she had already decided would be her new home. "What do you think?" She spread her arms and spun around in the living room.

"Give me a chance to look around first, Bronze." An out-of-breath Stephanie surveyed the apartment, visiting each room with Bronze eagerly at her heels. The large rooms and the hardwood floors buffed to a deep shine impressed Stephanie. She was particularly partial to the large living room window overlooking the park. She could already imagine Bronze at the window seat curled up with a good book. The kitchen, though spacious enough for a full-sized dinette set, would look nice with that small bar stool and table set she spotted in the Ikea catalog just the other day. She made a note to purchase it for her daughter as a housewarming gift. The bathroom was small but efficient, and Stephanie was certain that with a good paint job and the right curtains to add some color, coupled with a few cozy and inviting towels and other bathroom accessories, it would lose that mundane look. The bedrooms, located in the rear of the apartment, boasted of large closets and oatmeal-colored wall-to-wall carpeting.

"So what do you think, Ma?"

She looked at her daughter and nodded her approval. "With the right touches it could look like home."

"I knew you'd love it too! I think we should go see the landlord so I can sign on the dotted line."

"Did you bring your checkbook?"

"I sure did!" she exclaimed whipping her wallet from her purse."

"Well, I suppose you have a check to write then."

Bronze was elated and hugged Stephanie tightly. "Thanks, Ma."

Fifteen minutes later, Bronze walked out of 379 Holloman Way with lease in hand. She and her mother stopped by Ooh Cannolis to celebrate with a sweet, creamy treat.

Bronze was thrilled to be on her own, though she knew missing her mother would be an understatement. It was a bittersweet time in her life. She longed for her independence and space, but at the same time she dreaded the thought of her mother's imagined loneliness. What she failed to realize was that although she would be missed, Stephanie's world would not end. After all, a parent raises a child to let her go. Sure the house would be quiet, and many meals would be eaten at a table set for one, but Stephanie would survive. She explained this to her daughter on their last night under the same roof together.

"Don't worry about me, Bronze. I'm only a phone call away, and you know it'll take more than distance to separate us." Then she laughed. "You'll probably be so busy entertaining your friends you won't have time to worry about your momma. And thank goodness I won't have to put up with your blow-drying past midnight anymore." She paused and looked pensively at her daughter. "I'm proud of you, Bronze." Stephanie fingered Bronze's hair as if she were still a small child. Her baby was all grown up. "Do you know how many adult children move back home permanently? We'll both be fine. You'll see."

Bronze continued to work her butt off in overtime, anxious to furnish her new home. She could very easily have asked her mother for a loan, but opted not to. Bronze always preferred using her hard-earned money as opposed to money loaned or received as a gift. Even in college, Bronze would freely spend her earnings and deposit the funds that Stephanie sent to her. In fact, she couldn't bring herself to touch Stephanie's money until it had adequate time to "rub shoulders" with her own banked funds before being withdrawn.

Little by little Bronze was able to buy the needed furnishings for her apartment. She was knocked off her feet on the day Stephanie's housewarming gift arrived. It came as a totally unexpected surprise, and the delivery men were nice enough to assemble the set for her.

On Saturday evenings she and Stephanie would frequent malls and warehouses. Bronze could not always articulate precisely what she wanted, but when she laid eyes on it, something would click, which is how she furnished her home, by clicks. Her most significant piece of furniture was her stereo. She would come home after a particularly draining day at Hubert's, collapse on her vanilla sofa, and be massaged back to sanity by the elixir-like qualities of music and a foot soak.

One Friday night Bronze invited Brandon, Angela,

and Angela's new beau over to assemble her entertainment center. This gave her the chance to meet Angela's latest. All she knew was that he had started working at First Morgan Trust about a year after she was laid off.

Brandon arrived first. He was happy to see Bronze and not afraid to show it. He kissed her deeply.

"Are we alone?"

"Yes."

"Good." He was glad to have her all to himself. He grabbed her by the waist, pulled her close and pecked her on the lips.

"Hungry?" she asked pulling away from his embrace. She checked the food in the oven, decided to give the lasagna a few more minutes, and carried the fresh veggies and dip into the living room. Brandon followed, grabbing her from behind.

"When are you going to stop teasing me, Bronze?" he asked. "We both know it's just a matter of time. Let's get this party started."

Bronze wasn't certain if the rising heat was a result of the oven or desire. Probably a little of both. An old joke from high school popped into her head; she tried to stifle a giggle between the kisses.

"What's so funny?"

"Why is a woman like an oven? Because she gets hot before the meat goes in."

"I bet you're a real freak." He put her hand on his hard-on. "Think you can handle it?" he asked.

"Bring it on! The question is, can you handle me?"

Just then the doorbell rang, further delaying the game.

Angela entered first. "Hey, what's up? Bronze, Brandon, this is Jeff Pierce." Jeff was a well-built, light-skinned man with cute dimples. He looked to be no more than nineteen years old. Brandon extended a hand and the men shook.

"Have a seat. Can I get you anything to drink?" Bronze asked.

"No, I'm good," Jeff said, wasting no time to snack from the vegetable tray. He dipped a stalk of celery into the cup of ranch dressing.

Bronze and Angela headed for the kitchen while Brandon and Jeff stayed in the living room.

"So what do you think?" Angela asked.

"That you robbed the cradle. How old is he?" Bronze whispered.

"Twenty."

"In some states he wouldn't even be legal."

"And thank goodness this ain't one of them." They both laughed above the stereo and the voices of the men in the other room.

"How'd you meet him?"

"At the gym. We were scoping each other, and he invited me out for drinks. I figured what the heck. He's a tenderoni. Why not? You know me. So we went out, and so far it's been clickin'."

"Does the age difference bother you?" Bronze asked.

"Six years? Not when I think of the perks. He can put his tartar sauce on my fish sandwich anytime."

"Ugh! Fish, huh? Girl, I got a douche in the bathroom you can use right now! Come to think of it, I've got a few of them; you can take one with you!" They burst into laughter a second time.

"We're just two people having a good time for as long as it lasts," Angela said matter-of-factly. "You and Brandon look cozy."

"I could really fall for this man," Bronze said, giving a slightly alarmed look. "Girl, I gotta watch myself. If you and Jeff hadn't have gotten here when you did, yall may have been knocking on the door for a little while, 'cause we were in here about to be knocking something else," she winked.

Angela nearly spit her drink out trying not to laugh. She wiped her mouth with a napkin, giggling. "So what's up with that last G? The brotha got at least two of 'em."

"You don't hear me complaining do you?"

"Well, did you give him some yet?"

"No, but I have an appointment with the gynecologist next week, I'm back on the Pill." Bronze said.

"Remember the first time you went to the coochie doctor, you begged him to use the tiniest cervical dilator?" Angela recalled.

"Un-huh! And then on the next visit that thing was in and out before I even knew it." They both burst out laughing.

"Girrrl, you had that corn bread-fed buck to thank for that. What was his name again?" Angela asked.

"Carlon. The bum. All he was good for was one thing." She closed her eyes reminiscing the good part of what he offered, then crossed her legs exaggeratedly.

"Well, I guess everybody has to be good at something."

Two hours later the entertainment center was completely assembled and Bronze's television, DVD/VCR player, and music system were in place. Having eaten while they worked, Brandon and Jeff collected the plates and glasses from the coffee table, and took them to the kitchen. The men returned and Brandon took a seat on the sofa next to Bronze.

"The food was delicious, Bronze," he stated out loud, but then pulled her close to whisper in her ear. "And when your company leaves, you're gonna be my dessert."

"Don't write a check your mouth can't cash," she whispered back, rolling her eyes seductively.

"You forget I have a full line of credit." Brandon didn't bother to whisper this time.

"Speaking of finances," Jeff said, "You know I'm on your old j-o-b, right, Bronze?"

"Oh yeah, Angela was telling me that you're working at the bank," she said.

"Do you remember Christine Barrington?" Jeff asked.

"Yeah. Miss Got Rocks Wilcox," Bronze said.

"Exactly. You'll never guess who she's sweatin'."

"Who?"

"Nicholas Hall."

"Wait a minute. Nicholas Hall? From the loan department? Get outta here. I used to work with his sister, Monique. She must be seeing red. And I bet Daddy Big Bucks is having conniptions."

"They say Papa Cash is ready to disown her if she doesn't cut him loose," Jeff added.

"Sounds like the brother's taking care of business." Brandon grinned.

"No doubt. You know it's good to her if she's even *thinking* about giving up the Benjamin's for him. Talk about dick on the brain!" Jeff was blunt. Bronze cut her eyes to Angela with raised eyebrows as if to say 'No this little boy ain't using grown folk's words!' "But let *us* think with our dicks and they wanna castrate us. You see how you women contradict yourselves?"

"Yeah, they wanna hang a brother for being hung. Ain't that a blip?

But let me tell you something about women, Jeff," Brandon said. "Stop trying to analyze them because they don't even understand themselves. Just go with the flow."

"Yeah, you're right, man," Jeff agreed.

"Puhleez. Give me a break," Angela said. "We are more in tune with ourselves than you brothers will *ever* be."

"That's bull. How many times has a woman said no and meant yes?" Jeff asked Angela.

"Well, you won't be getting none tonight, that's for sure. So don't get it twisted," Angela said.

"Trust me. By the time I get you home you'll be begging for it!" Jeff winked at Angela.

"So what's up for the weekend?" Angela asked, changing the subject.

"Anybody seen Martin Lawrence's new comedy?" Brandon asked.

"Let's all go tomorrow night." Bronze looked at the three of them.

"I'm down," Jeff said.

"Sounds like a plan. Bronze, Brandon, it's getting late. We're gonna hit the road. I promised my sister I'd return her DVD before Blockbuster closes." Angela stood.

"Nice meeting you, man." Jeff shook Brandon's hand.

"Same here. See you tomorrow."

"Thanks for your help, Jeff." Bronze smiled.

"Okay, babe, talk to you tomorrow," Angela said, kissing Bronze's cheek.

"Get home safely." Bronze closed the door behind them.

"Do you want me to spend the night?" Brandon asked.

"I know you think I'm just a tease, but can we take a rain check?"

"Does no mean yes?"

"Boy, that question must be etched in the male brain."

"Oh, you mean Jeff? Sometimes men like aggravating women before they sleep with them."

"On purpose? Why?" Bronze felt naïve.

"It makes for better screwing. Everything tightens up."

"Tell me more." Bronze folded her arms across her chest and waited for Brandon to continue.

"I can't divulge *all* the secrets. I've told you too much already, and I'd rather show you than tell you," he said, bringing his hand up to cup her breast. "I promise to make it worth your while."

She rubbed her knee against his thigh and kissed him like she never had before. Brandon's hands were hot on her haltered back. She let out a soft moan and slowly unzipped his jeans. It was going to be a good night.

He pulled away slowly and zipped his jeans back up. "Keep it on simmer, sweetheart. I'll be back."

Bronze learned another male mantra that night: make 'em beg for it.

Chapter 15

As usual Dr. Whitney's waiting room was busy. Two young women were first-time visitors filling out medical questionnaires on clipboards while Dr. Whitney's ten-fifteen walked through the door. Bronze's appointment wasn't until 10:45, but she always arrived early for her doctor's appointments. Sometimes it paid off. Today was not one of those days. Bronze did not get into the stirrups until 11:30, and it was another ten minutes before she finally saw her gynecologist.

Dr. Whitney was a tall, well-built middle-aged man who must have been something else in his day. She secretly enjoyed their visits and being the object of his easy charm. He looked over her chart before the exam.

"It's been almost a year since your last visit, Bronze. Been celibate, have you?"

"Sort of."

"Sort of? Is that like ending up sort of pregnant?"

"No, but the relationship wasn't going anywhere so I figured why pop all those hormones."

"Screw up, did he? Excuse the pun."

"It wasn't his fault. I was just lonely and horny," Bronze admitted.

"Lonely? Horny? You mean no one decent out there has been pulling your coattail? Hell, if I were thirty years younger, I'd take you on myself. As much as you have going for you. Are you kidding? Look, buy a puppy and a vibrator. They're safer. I hope you at least used those female condoms I gave you."

"Yes, Dr. Whitney, along with the spermicide."

"Good girl. Now let's see what's going on here," Dr. Whitney said, putting on his latex gloves.

Twenty minutes later, Bronze was seated in Dr. Whitney's office fully dressed. He wrote her a prescription for contraceptives, and she promised to see him again in six months.

Bronze began taking her birth control pills and soon after invited Brandon into her bed. She and Brandon had been teasing each other for over a month, and she was ready to take their relationship to the next level. She planned a romantic, candlelight dinner for them, which would lead to other things. It was a Saturday evening that Bronze found herself busy in the kitchen, humming up a storm as she prepared their special meal of broiled shell steak, angel hair pasta, and garden salad. She didn't want anything too heavy for their intimate evening, nothing to weigh them down. She almost decided against the chocolate blackout cake. Almost.

She didn't know how she'd gotten through the day. Her mind had been on nothing but Brandon's taut, brown body and the pleasure it would bring her. Between customers she made a mental note of what she'd serve in and out of the bedroom. Brandon Wilde—her brass bed's first guest. How long had they been teasing each other? They both knew from jump street where they'd end up. But sometimes it was more fun taking the scenic route and tantalizing each other until neither could stand it any longer. They had reached that point, and there was no turning back.

The glass coffee table was set. She decided to have dinner by candlelight in the living room on two large pillows. She didn't want to be stuck in the kitchen listening to a leaky faucet. Bronze checked her watch. She had just enough time to bathe and change into something comfortably sexy. She chose a wine colored lace chemise that barely covered her behind. It came with matching tanga panties that tied on each side for easy removal, which was exactly what Bronze wanted.

At 8:04 Bronze was seated at her kitchen table drumming her fingers and wondering where the heck Brandon was. He was already half an hour late. She heard a car door slam. *Oh, God, he's here!* She ran to the bathroom mirror making certain that her hair and makeup were just so. She dabbed Forever between her cleavage and thighs, and a bit more behind her ears.

The doorbell rang. Bronze greeted Brandon with a warm smile and a glass of champagne. His eyes nearly popped out of their sockets while he accepted the drink. "Let me take your coat," she said closing the door behind him. As she turned to hang his coat in the closet, Brandon took full advantage of eyeing her ass peeking from the hemline of her chemise. Although there were hangers available on the bar in the closet, Bronze bent at the waist to retrieve one from the floor, allowing Brandon a full view.

"Damn, girl!" he commented.

"How was your day?" she asked turning slowly towards him.

"Put it like this. I spent half the day helping my cousin fix his car and the other half getting all that motor oil and gook from under my nails. But shit, you done made me forget all about that." His eyes were focused on her erect nipples that poked into the lace.

"Let's see." She examined his hands. She took the flute from him, dipped his middle finger into the glass, then sucked his fingertip as she coaxed Brandon to take a seat on the sofa. "They look fine to me." She climbed atop him in a straddle, enjoying the pleasure in her groin as his manhood pressed forward to meet her. They were just a fraction of an inch apart—eye to eye, mouth to mouth, breasts to chest. She felt his breath on her face. Their eyes locked, and then his mouth covered hers. He reached for the warm moistness between her legs. Six weeks of pent-up passion boiled down to that moment. With a quick hand, he maneuvered her panties aside and slid one finger inside her. Bronze exhaled so quickly and heavily, she startled herself. She rotated her hips against his hand while he dropped his head to her breasts, still covered by the chemise, and began to feast.

Suddenly nothing mattered. Not the champagne, the dinner, nor the music. Two minutes later their clothing didn't matter either. The only thing that mattered was them. His erection bulged and throbbed, beckoning her and begging for her at the same time. He swooped her up in his arms and carried her into the bedroom. Once there, he gently lowered her to the bed, but not before his eyes beheld the single red rose that she had placed on his pillow.

"For me?" he asked.

"It's all for you."

"I'm gonna hold you to that," he said easing the chemise up her body and over her head.

"I wouldn't have it any other way."

He kissed her cheeks, her neck, and each breast. "Damn, Bronze," he said under his breath, "I've been waiting so long for this. Is it mine? Tell me it's mine."

"It's yours, baby. It's all yours. Take it," she whispered.

He turned her over onto her stomach, massaging her shoulders and then her back. He made her feel so damn good. She closed her eyes, relishing every moment, every touch. He kissed her down her back, then to her butt, then to her thighs, but not to where she really wanted him. Instead, he continued downwards to the back of her knee, down her calf, and to her ankle.

"Brandon," she called out. He slid up her body and allowed his weight to fall against her back.

"Shhhh." He kissed her on the ear and positioned his firmness between her legs, allowing his head to tease her at her hot entrance. Unable to take anymore of his erotic torture, she pushed up and turned over to her back, then wrapped her legs around his waist. He dove again to her breasts, which seemed to be staring straight up at him. In sheer anticipation of what awaited her, Bronze grasped a handful of sheet and pulled it towards her, only letting go to pull Brandon away from her boobs and kiss him deeply. She couldn't get her tongue far enough into his mouth. She grabbed him by the butt.

He knew she was ready. "Shit!" he said.

"What's wrong?"

"Be right back." It only took a moment for him to return with condoms in hand and another minute before one was on. But she couldn't wait any longer.

"Brandon, please."

"Shhhh." He entered her.

"Ooh," she moaned. It was so damn good. So good. He moved rhythmically and skillfully and Bronze fit easily into his groove. It wasn't long before she felt herself approaching that marvelous relief. "Oh, Brandon, I'm cumming." She couldn't hold him close enough. Soon he was grunting and moaning, too, then gently collapsed on top of her.

"You are so damn sexy, lady," he panted. She smiled and ran her hand over his head.

"For a minute I thought you had forgotten your raincoat."

"And miss all this?" He rolled off of her and settled himself on a pillow. "Come here," he said softly, cuddling and kissing her.

"We did this backwards. We were supposed to have dinner first and then dessert," Bronze said.

"Disappointed?"

"Not hardly," she said, laughing. "Let's go eat!" She threw on a nightshirt and gave him her white terry robe.

Bronze warmed up their dinner, and they ate by candlelight as she had originally planned. "So tell me, Mr. Wilde, was I worth the wait? Wait, don't answer that until you taste my chocolate cake." She came over, sat in his lap, and spooned some into his mouth. "What do you think?"

He let the smooth creaminess slide down his throat before answering. "You tell me." He lifted up her nightshirt and spread some frosting on her breasts with his forefinger.

Bronze held her breath as Brandon sucked chocolate off her nipples. "Mmm, nice," she moaned. She blew out the candles. "Let's go back to bed!"

Early Sunday morning Angela's phone rang, jarring her back into consciousness. She checked her clock radio on the nightstand: 7:24. Who could be calling her at this hour?

"Hello?"

"Angela, this is Jagger Melrose. Did I wake you?"

How ludicrous, she thought. *I'm always up at this hour on Sundays*. "Not at all."

"Good. Have you looked at your advance copy of *Candor*?"

"Not yet, Mr. Melrose."

"Well, give me a call when you do. I'm at the office." And with that he hung up.

What could be so freaking important at seven in the morning? She got out of bed and put on her robe. Her early-morning apartment was always a little chilly. The copy of *Candor* was on her kitchen table just as she had left it Friday evening, where she'd placed all the mail.

She made herself a cup of coffee and proceeded to read the magazine. Actress Simone Russell and her family were on the cover. The sister had a tough haircut tapered in the back and asymmetric in front. Hair was the first thing Angela noticed about a person. Perhaps because she paid so much attention to her own.

"Let's see Fashion, Politics, Sports, Beauty, Features . . . 'In Home Shopping—the New Trend' by Debbie Wilson; 'When Bi Doesn't Mean So Long' by Angela Sommers."

"Oh my goodness." she reached for her coffee mug. Quickly she flipped to page forty-six. The familiar piece on male bisexuality began with a scenario of a woman who eyes a man from across the room at a party. He's scoping her too, or so she thinks. *Here he comes,* she says to herself, flashing that knowing smile. But wait, there he goes! Straight to that fine-looking brother by the bar.

She dialed the office.

"Yes, Angela." Jagger picked up on the first ring.

"Did you see it?" she practically screamed into the phone, her voice clothed in excitement. "I don't believe it!"

"Well, believe it. You did it. Congratulations."

"Thank you so much, Mr. Melrose."

"You deserved it, Angela. See you tomorrow."

Angela hung up the phone absolutely ecstatic. "Yessss!" Angela could not dial her parents' phone number fast enough.

John and Laura Sommers were proud of their youngest daughter's accomplishment. "Baby girl, I knew you could do it. Here, let me put your mother on."

"Hi, Angie. Daddy and I are so proud of you. When can we read it?"

"How about later this afternoon?" Angela asked.

"Okay. Why don't you come over for dinner? I'll fix your favorite—roast beef and cabbage."

"Great, I'll be over about six. Tell Daddy good-bye."

"Okay. See you then, Angie."

Next Angela called Bronze. "Wake up, sleepyhead. I got good news."

"Oh yeah? That makes two of us. Tell me your news first."

So Angela told Bronze all about her article. "I know Julian put you through the wringer, but I hope you're not mad at me for writing this article."

"Of course not, and I love that title. You know we gotta celebrate, right?" Bronze insisted.

"Of course. Now let's hear your good news."

"Let's just say me and Brandon did a little sumthin' sumthin' last night."

"Well, it's about time. How long has it been for you anyway? Eleven months?"

"No, eleven looong months. Let's get it right, now." They both laughed.

"Hey, let's go out for breakfast."

"Okay, sounds good. Listen, pick me up about ten-thirty. That way I'll go straight to work from there."

"All right. See you then."

Brandon had slept in his own bed last night. As much as he had wanted to stay with Bronze, his better judgment warned against it. Women were funny. Spend one night with them, and they think they own you. They were ready to rearrange your sock drawer. Maybe Bronze would be different, but he didn't want to risk it. Not the first night anyway. He could already tell that she was wife material.

As he got out of the shower the telephone rang. He ran to answer it, leaving a trail of water behind him. Bronze must have gotten the flowers he'd sent her, he thought as he answered the phone.

"Hello?" he said in his sexiest voice, knowing already who was on the other end without checking the caller id.

"You're sure in a good mood."

Damn, it was Capricia. What did she want? "What can I do for you, Capricia?"

"Relax, Brandon. This is business, not pleasure. And besides, I'm five hundred miles away so you're safe."

Brandon chose to ignore that last remark.

"I'm having trouble with my computer, and I need some help."

"Look, you're in Atlanta. Don't tell me Ohio is the only place you can call for help."

"No, but I wanted that personal touch. Don't be mad at me, Brandon," she said softly. "You know we'll always share a bond. Let's call a truce. Besides, you owe me lunch the next time I'm in town."

"And when will that be?"

"Whenever you want it to be."

Brandon heard the call waiting tone on his phone. Thank heavens for small miracles. "Hold on, Capricia. Someone's on the other line."

"No, I'll talk to you later. Think about what I said, Brandon. It doesn't have to be over." And with that she hung up.

"Hello, Brandon. The roses are beautiful."

"My pleasure; you're beautiful." He could almost hear Bronze blush. "Listen, what are you doing today?"

"I'm working twelve to five, but Angela and I are going out to breakfast. We're celebrating. You know she finally got her byline."

"Yeah, I read the advance copy Friday. I know she must be on cloud nine. Hey, why don't I pick you up after work?" Brandon suggested.

"Sure. I'll see you later then."

* * *

Bronze and Angela decided to eat at the Pancake Inn a few miles from the mall. From the moment Angela picked up Bronze, she noticed a change in her friend. Something around the eyes. Something she had seen once or twice in her own mirror. It was the look of a satisfied woman after a long drought. She said as much to Bronze over breakfast.

"Get outta here."

"No, I'm serious. You're much more relaxed. You'd be surprised how uptight and anxious sex—or the lack of it—can make you feel and look. Hmmm, maybe my next article will be about sexual deprivation."

"That's one way to get a reputation quick. Everybody'll think all you think about is sex."

"Well it's certainly good for the circulation."

"Yours or the magazines?"

"Both," Angela said, smiling.

"I hope you brought the article for me to read."

"But of course," she said taking the issue of *Candor* from her bag, treating it like the prized possession it was.

Bronze ate with the article by her side, her attention divided between the magazine and her plate. Finally, she finished both.

"So what d'ya think, honestly?" Angela asked.

"I'm impressed. I mean I could have read this same article in *Essence* or *Cosmopolitan*. You did good!"

"Thanks. You did too. Brandon's quite a catch."

"As if I didn't know," Bronze agreed.

"I can't tell you how many women at work have the hots for him."

"Is he interested in any of them?"

"Not really. He was seeing some girl from accounting for a while. But he hasn't gone nuts over anyone since some chick he brought to the Christmas party a couple of years ago—Capricia something. Until you came along, that is."

"What was she like?"

"Miss Thang? Tall with short black hair, with an ass that could knock down a cinder block wall." Bronze frowned, suddenly wondering if she was any competition for Brandon's ex. "Girl, her front side would step off the elevator a full five minutes before her backside made it off; it was just nasty! She's in Atlanta now working for her uncle—some congressman or something. Talk about nepotism."

"I wonder why they split."

"Don't know, don't care. She's history."

"He's picking me up after work later. We better get going if I'm gonna make it to work on time."

"Yeah," Angela agreed. "Let's hit the road."

Chapter 16

As usual the retail industry reflected the approaching holiday season and Hubert's was no exception. The increased volume of customers was evident in every department, including cosmetics.

Normally, Sundays were slow—that is until November when the tempo picked up. Her manager promised that the holiday help would be arriving any day, but in the meantime, Bronze and the other girls had to take up the slack. Bronze worked her corns off in those few short hours that day. It was tiring, but on the other hand, the increase in Bronze's commission checks was nothing to sneeze at.

Nonetheless, Bronze could not wait until five o'clock came and she said as much to Jasmine West, who worked the Fragrance Bar, during their short break in the mall's food court.

"Hot date with Brandon later?" Jasmine asked in her Georgian twang.

"You got it. He's picking me up later."

"You know, he reminds me of someone," Jasmine revealed.

"Oh yeah? Who?"

"I don't know. I can't put my finger on it right now. Does he have any brothers?"

"No, just one sister."

"Well, give me time. It'll come to me."

"So what are you doing tonight?" Bronze asked.

"Oh, I have a date with a bubble bath."

"We do too. He just doesn't know it yet." Bronze winked.

"Ooooh! Bronze, I knew you were a little freak." They both laughed.

"I know what I wanted to ask you. Do you have any Forever bath gel samples? That scent drives Brandon wild!"

"No, but there's a GWP going on right now."

"What do I have to buy?"

"Nothing. The line girl always gets a free GWP. I'll just give you mine. That's all."

"Jazz, you're a sweetie." Bronze smiled.

"Hey, anything for the cause."

Bronze glanced at her watch. "We better get back."

They finished their sodas and returned to Hubert's. By that time it was 3:30 and things began to quiet down. Bronze recorded the rest of her cosmetic inventory though she was interrupted more times than she cared to be. After which, she began addressing postcards to her regular customers, advising them of Velvet's upcoming promotions, which would be available in just two weeks, the day after Thanksgiving. This was always Velvet's biggest promotion of the year, and the inventory was due in the following week. Halfway through addressing the postcards the phone rang. It was Brandon.

"Bronze, I'm glad I caught you. Listen, I got called

in to the office on an emergency, and it doesn't look like I'll be able to pick you up. I'm hoping I'll be finished within the next hour or so, and I can just head on over to your apartment. Otherwise, I'll have to take a rain check."

"Don't worry about it. Actually, I'm a little tired. We were up pretty late last night. If you get off early, give me a call. If not, I'll talk to you tomorrow."

"Sorry, Bronze. I was really looking forward to seeing you tonight."

"Don't worry about it," she said, not letting it become an issue, although she was disappointed.

It had been quite a while since Stephanie had seen her daughter. She made a special effort not to be a clinging, demanding mother. Nonetheless, she was delighted when Bronze stopped by Sunday evening bearing cheesecake.

"Have you eaten, hon?" Stephanie asked as they settled in the kitchen.

"No, Brandon and I had made plans, but he had to cancel at the last minute."

"Well, fix yourself a plate. How's he doing anyway?"

"Fine, just working hard. I'm back on the pill."

"Well, excuse me!" Stephanie knew that her daughter cared a lot about Brandon. She also knew that Brandon seemed to be a very level-headed guy. At least that's the impression she got from the few times she'd met him. "Well, I hope you two are careful."

"Don't worry, Ma, we are." Bronze sat at the table ready to dig into her plate of meatloaf, mashed potatoes and gravy, sweet peas, and salad.

Stephanie couldn't help smiling as she watched Bronze eat. As a child, Bronze only ate sweet peas if they were covered in a mountain of mashed potatoes. How long had it taken her to outgrow that habit? This was the same little girl who climbed up on her mother's lap and asked about her father. Stephanie knew that though she only asked once, the question burned in Bronze's heart.

Stephanie didn't know where to begin. She could still hear her mother's voice in her ear pleading with her. "Bronze has got to know the truth. She deserves to know. My goodness, Stephanie, you've kept this secret for twenty-five years, and the Lord has been kind. But, my dear, if she hears it from a total stranger, you may lose your daughter. Think about it." What had Stephanie's mother always said? The truth will come out. No. The truth will *always* come out. Stephanie promised her mother that she would tell Bronze the truth.

"Ma, you seem preoccupied," Bronze said, interrupting her mother's thoughts. "What's up?"

"I talked to your grandmother today. She sends her love."

"I owe her a call. How is she?"

"You know your grandmother; just as spunky as ever. But her arthritis has been acting up. She asked about Brandon and how you two were doing."

Try as she might, Stephanie could not think of a way to broach the subject. It was as though she blinked and twenty-five years passed. Where did she start? Bronze was the most precious part of her life, and the mere thought of jeopardizing their relationship was excruciating. Yet, Stephanie knew that her mother was right. Sooner or later Bronze would have to be told the truth.

But right now, the words stuck in her throat. She'd have to pray over it some more and ask the Lord to give her the strength to choose the right words to say at the right time.

"I think I'll have some cheesecake now," Bronze said, finishing her dinner. "Want some?" She waited for an answer that did not come. "Ma?"

"What's that, honey?"

"I said do you want some cheesecake?"

"Sure. Cut me a nice big piece." Stephanie needed something to make herself feel better, no matter how temporary the fix.

Chapter 17

Thanksgiving Day at Stephanie's was truly a feast. Amid the turkey and dressing, the Sutton clan gathered for the start of the holiday season. They made up for lost time since they had not all been together since Vanessa's summer wedding. The sounds of joking and laughter could be heard over the clinking of silverware against china, and the aroma of a smorgasbord of delectable foods filled the air.

Even Stephanie's friend Leo Stone stopped by. Leo was a widower. He and Stephanie had been seeing each other on and off for about two years.

As expected, the newlyweds, Vanessa and Dave, were the last to arrive, and the big news of the evening was their announcement. They were expecting an addition to the family. Only one month pregnant, Vanessa was glowing. Everyone was thrilled at the news.

"But do you think it's too soon, Grandma?" Vanessa asked looking pensively at Rose. "I mean we've only been married a few months," Vanessa said.

"Nonsense," Rose replied. "You'll have a baby when

the Good Lord wants you to, whether it's nine months into your marriage or nine years."

"Relax, Vee," her sister Melissa added. "You've got a ring on your finger. What do you care what other people think?"

"I couldn't have said it better myself, Melissa," Rose agreed.

By the time dessert rolled around they were all stuffed, but no one could pass up Stephanie's homemade apple pie or Bronze's butter pound cake.

"Aunt Steph, you put your big toe into this pie." Dave loved it.

"Thank you, Dave. Have some more."

"No, I better stop while I'm ahead," he answered. Just then the doorbell rang.

"I'll get it," Bronze called out as she left her seat. "Hi, honey." Bronze welcomed Brandon inside. He gave her a quick kiss on the lips.

"You're cold." She shivered.

"Yeah, the hawk's out tonight," he said, giving her a bottle of wine.

"Let me take your coat. You remember my mother."

"Of course. How are you, Ms. Sutton?"

"Fine, Brandon. Good to see you again. Come on in."

Bronze introduced him to her family.

"Pull up a chair, Brandon. You're just in time for dessert. Bronze tells me you work for *Candor* magazine. You know, I still have their very first issue from fifty years ago," Rose said proudly.

"Oh yeah? I'd love to see that," Brandon admitted.

"Well next time we're all together, I'll be sure to bring it along. Or if you and Bronze come my way, we can take a trip up to the attic. You wouldn't believe the stuff one can accumulate after seventy-five years on this earth."

"Great. I'd like that." Brandon said.

"Hey, let's get a bid whist game going. Brandon, do you play?" Stephanie asked.

"Are you kidding? That's all we could afford to do in college on the weekends. Bronze, do you play?" Brandon asked.

"Uh-huh."

"She's the one who taught me. She and Angela," Stephanie said.

Bronze got the decks of cards from the kitchen, and Dave put up the card tables. Rose and Brandon against Melissa and Bronze at one table, while Stephanie and Vanessa partnered against Dave and Stephanie's brother Xavier.

For the next few hours all that could be heard over Grover Washington Jr. and Najee was uptown, downtown, which suit was trump, and who couldn't make their books. Rose surprised them all. At her age, her mind was as sharp and alert as the rest of them. And she never once reneged.

Somewhere after midnight they decided to call it an evening. Everyone was off the following day except for Bronze. The day after Thanksgiving was the biggest shopping day of the year, and almost everyone in the retail business was required to work.

Bronze said her good-byes while Brandon warmed the car. "When are you all going back to Havenwood?" Bronze asked her visiting family members.

"Tomorrow afternoon," Uncle Xavier said.

"Well, have a safe trip back home." She hugged each of them and gave Vanessa a little pat on her stomach. Bronze gave her grandmother a special embrace. Rose whispered into her granddaughter's ear, "I like your young man. You got him hooked, now you just have to reel 'im in. If you need some advice, let me know," she said, smiling.

"I'll remember that, Grandma," Bronze said.

Chapter 18

The day that Hubert's and all other retailers looked forward to all year long, finally arrived. And to get a head start on the shoppers, Hubert's opened promptly at six. Lines had formed at all the entrances, and customers eager to unload cash and have their magic plastic massaged couldn't enter fast enough.

Bronze made her first sale at three minutes after the store opened, followed almost immediately by two other transactions. She could tell the type of day she'd be having, especially with the Velvet gift baskets on display. They included eau de parfum, lotion, powder, and bath gel. Men, particularly, loved buying them for their wives or sweethearts because it took the guesswork out of shopping.

There was no denying the excitement in the air and that, along with the giant wreaths and Christmas ornaments suspended from the ceiling, only added to the festive mood. Women from all the major fragrance houses were busy spritzing customers with perfume and handing out samples. As a result, the Fragrance Bar and the Velvet counter was bombarded with customers. In fact, Bronze had been so busy working that she lost all track of time. It was only after Jasmine came to get her that she realized it was lunchtime.

"Let's get outta here," Bronze said. "Now I see why people smoke."

They had to wait longer than usual for a table in the food court because of all the extra holiday traffic. It never ceased to amaze Bronze that no matter how much people ate on Thanksgiving, they were always ready to chow down on junk food less than twenty-four hours later. God bless Mickey D's. Finally, they were seated with their lunch before them.

"You know, it finally came to me," Jasmine began.

"What's that?" Bronze asked, taking a bite out of her burger.

"Who Brandon reminds me of."

"That's right. You did say he looked familiar."

"He reminds me of that other guy who used to come by and take you to lunch."

"What other guy?" Bronze thought for a moment. "Wait a minute, you mean Julian?"

"Yeah, that's the one!"

"Where? In his big toe? Get outta here!" Bronze dismissed the notion with a quick flick of her wrist.

"I'm serious, Bronze. They could be related. They look alike."

"I don't think so. Brandon is tall, brown, and handsome. And—"

"And Julian is too. Stop and think a minute, Bronze," Jasmine told her, taking another bite of her pizza.

"Nah, that's totally ridiculous," Bronze said, laughing.

"Okay, well forget I brought it up. We better get back before Melba calls the National Guard out on us."

Angela and the rest of Jagger Melrose's small staff returned to their department after the general staff meeting was adjourned. They were all abuzz with the news: *Candor* was starting a new magazine for the African-American woman, and a contest was being held for the naming of this new publication.

Angela barely heard anything that Jagger said that morning. She was so engrossed in naming the new magazine. She shared her thoughts with Brandon over lunch.

"Did you see this coming?" she asked.

"You mean the new magazine? No. Management did one helluva job keeping this idea hush. But you know what it is. *Essence* really has no competition, and *Candor*'s decided it wants a piece of the pie. This is America. Economics is the name of the game."

"Speaking of economics, how's your Christmas shopping going?" she asked.

"If you're talking about for Bronze, I'm racking my brains. Any suggestions?"

"How about gold?" Angela asked. "She adores jewelry."

"I thought about that. Actually, I saw this beautiful amethyst ring in the window of Miller's Jewelers. A real eye catcher, and I know she'd love it."

"So what's the problem?" Angela asked.

"My father always says, don't buy a woman a ring unless you've already bought her *the* ring."

"Well, how do you feel about Bronze?"

"I'm crazy about her. And I don't want to jinx our relationship."

"Then I guess you've answered your own question," Angela said simply.

Chapter 19

Bronze zapped the snooze button and lay in bed for a few extra minutes after her alarm clock went off. Another Saturday in December, which only meant one thing: Hubert's would be swamped. For a moment she toyed with the idea of calling in, but changed her mind. She could rack up in commission on days like this. Plus, she'd be off tomorrow to recuperate.

Bronze looked at the picture of Brandon on the dresser. Whatever gave Jasmine the idea that he and Julian looked alike? She got out of bed and picked the photo up, closely examining Brandon's face. Objectively. She even saw the tiny scar on his nose. He had gotten it when he fell out of his tree house at twelve years old. Brandon and Julian were the same height and build, but that's where the similarities ended. Bronze showered, grabbed a quick breakfast, and headed for Hubert's.

That evening after work Bronze browsed through her closet for something to wear to *Candor*'s upcoming Christmas party. Brandon had called her earlier in the day to invite her, and she wanted to look stunning for the occasion. The party was in two weeks, but she didn't want to wait until the last minute to find something to wear.

She called Angela. "You know, I can't find a doggone thing to wear to your party."

"What about that gold lamè jacket and black velvet skirt?" she suggested. "You look sharp in that."

"Nah, I want something brand new. What are you wearing?"

"What am I wearing?" Angela repeated. "I might just skip it."

"Why? What's up?"

"Jeff and I broke up last night."

"And you're heartbroken enough to miss the company's Christmas party? What has gotten into you?" This was definitely out of Angela's relationship controlling nature. "What happened?" Bronze asked.

"Nothing, girl; He's sweatin' me. Girl, I can't even go to the bathroom without him trailing behind me. He wanted to move in, and I told him no. So he said we should stop seeing each other for a while and I called his bluff. Only he doesn't know that Angela doesn't go backward. When I'm through, I'm through."

"So what does that have to do with your not going to the party? Just find another date. I've seen you in action. That's never a problem for you."

"I'm not in that festive mood. And my period's a week late."

"Dag. Is it ever that late?"

"Nope. I made an appointment to see Dr. Whitney on Monday."

"Have you told anyone else?"

"Not a soul," Angela answered.

"What will you do if you're pregnant?"

"I don't know. I'll cross that bridge when and if I get there. Why don't we go shopping for your dress? Maybe it'll take my mind off my period. I mean, there's nothing I can do about it until I'm sure anyway. No sense worrying myself to death."

"Are you sure you feel up to it?"

"Yeah, I'm sure. Pick you up around seven-thirty?"

"Great."

Bronze and Angela drove out to Bloom Park Mall in search of what Bronze called an "eye-popping" dress. After six stores and one-and-a-half hours of shopping, Bronze stumbled upon *the* dress. It was a black velvet strapless number with a floor length, fishtailed hemline. She immediately tried it on.

"Absolutely stunning," Angela commented.

Bronze knew that the dress was out of her price range, but she handed the salesgirl her charge card before her mind talked her out of it. Thank goodness she already had high-heeled black velvet pumps and the perfect earrings at home.

"Brandon won't know what hit him when he sees you in that dress. I bet he won't let you out of his sight all night."

"That's the plan," she said, grinning.

Monday morning Angela had a nine o'clock appointment with Dr. Whitney. She told him about her suspicions, and he examined her thoroughly. He didn't think she was pregnant, but he ordered a pregnancy test for her anyway, just to ease her mind.

Chapter 20

Bronze couldn't get home from work fast enough that Thursday evening. Holiday traffic was heavy, and the bus just crawled along. She checked her watch. It was already after five, and she had so much to do before Brandon picked her up at seven for the *Candor* Christmas party.

Once home, she hurriedly ran her bubble bath and laid out her clothes on the bed. She was glad that she had just had a manicure a couple of days ago, and it was still intact. Although she didn't have time to bathe as long as she would have liked to, it was long enough to wash away the cares of the day, including the irate customer who returned, claiming that the new lipstick she had just bought had already been used. In actuality, she was returning it because she hadn't liked the way it looked on her after she had gotten it home. Who was she kidding?

Oh well, she thought as she soaked. *That's over with.*

By ten minutes till seven Bronze was ready. Brandon flipped when she answered the door. Her upswept hairdo, along with her bare shoulders and long neck, practically blew him away.

"Maybe we should have our own little party right here," he said, taking it all in.

"You like?"

"No question," he said simply.

The party was in full swing when Brandon and Bronze walked into the ballroom of the Hyatt Plaza Hotel. They spotted Angela and her date and joined them at their table.

Angela's first words were, "You look drop-dead gorgeous."

"You don't look so bad yourself, lady," Bronze said. Angela wore a purple cocktail dress trimmed in sequins around the plunging V back.

She introduced Bronze and Brandon to Keith Powell, her date for the evening. Bronze could tell that Angela was not impressed with Keith. She said as much to Angela when the guys went to get drinks for them.

"Okay. Where'd you find him?" Bronze wanted to know.

"My sister, Dee, fixed me up with him. They went to law school together. She claims he's the next Perry Mason, but he has no personality whatsoever. Ever since Dee got married, she's been into this security thing. I don't need no man to take care of me. I can take care of myself. But I do have some good news: I'm not pregnant."

"Thank God for that!"

"Yeah. Thank God, Jesus, and the entire heavenly host."

The men returned with their drinks and four small plates of hors d'oeuvres, one for each of them, in hand.

"Angela, are you working on your next byline?" Brandon asked.

"That and the name of the new magazine."

"Guess what they're thinking about giving away for the grand prize?"

"What?" Angela asked.

"A fifty-dollar savings bond."

"What? You mean they want me to rack my brains for fifty dollars?" She shook her head. "Wait a minute, can you earn royalties for naming a magazine? You're a lawyer, Keith. What do you think?"

"Not if they make you sign a release relinquishing all rights," Keith said. Angela gave some silent thought to his response. Bronze wasn't listening to the conversation. She was sitting across from Brandon, checking him out. He was wearing a charcoal, pinstriped, double-breasted suit and looked absolutely ravishing. What she wouldn't like to do to him right there at the table. Just thinking about it made her wet. As if reading her mind, Brandon looked over and winked at her. "Let's dance," he said simply.

"Enough shop talk," Angela decided. "It's time to party."

The deejay was playing *Dontchange* by Musiq. Bronze owned the CD and frequently played it when she came home from work after an extremely rough day. Sometimes she and Brandon made love to it. It was one of their songs.

The dance floor was getting crowded, but they were oblivious to the others. Brandon rubbed her bare shoulders, and she loved the warmth that it generated. There was something about a warm pair of hands on her back that drove her crazy. It was obvious to anyone watching them that they were in their own private world.

"Hey, lover boy, let me cut in. Let me cut in." Curtis Bratt from the research department slurred his words as he spoke, grabbing Brandon's shoulder from behind.

Brandon tried to ignore Curtis, but his persistence made it virtually impossible. He was like an annoying gnat, irritating and unwelcome.

"You sure can pick 'em, Wilde. Check out the gravy on them biscuits! Man, I could go for some of that." Liquor or no liquor, Curtis could be obnoxious when he wanted to be.

Brandon had had enough. "Just a second, Bronze." He grabbed Curtis by his collar and set him down in the nearest empty chair.

"Aaw, Brandon, I just wanna have some fun. That's all." Curtis was about as pathetic as a crippled cockroach. Several people had stopped dancing to observe the scene that Curtis was making.

Bronze and Brandon returned to their table. "What happened up there?" Angela asked.

"Curtis was just being Curtis," Brandon said simply.

"Say no more," Angela said.

The buffet dinner turned out to be a nice change from the usual sit-down routine. After eating, everyone was ready to boogie. Even Jagger and his wife were on the dance floor cutting a step.

"Remind me *never* to let my sister fix me up with anyone again," Angela said to Bronze as they headed to the ladies' lounge to freshen up. "Did you check out the guy with the gold bow tie?"

"Are you kidding? He's only been checking you out all night," Bronze said.

"That's Rod from photography. And I hear his is dipped in gold. He's been after me for months. I think I'm ready for a little sumthin' sumthin'."

"But for Keith's sake, not tonight."

"D'ya think Keith'll get the message if I stay in here long enough?"

"Now, Angela, be nice."

"Just a thought."

By the time Bronze and Angela left the lounge, they noticed another woman in Bronze's chair openly flirting with Brandon. "Wait a minute," Angela said. "You gotta watch Lauren. She's a slut deluxe. She's been trying to get her hooks in Brandon for a long time."

When they reached the table Lauren jumped up and blurted out, "Oh hi. You must be Capricia."

"Bitch," Angela said under her breath.

"Actually, I'm Bronze," she stately politely.

"I could have sworn Brandon told me his woman's name was Capricia. My bad." She laughed. Just then the deejay put on another slow jam.

"Sweetheart, let's dance." Bronze whisked off a relieved Brandon, leaving an envious Lauren behind.

Chapter 21

Christmas morning found Bronze awake at the crack of dawn. Brandon had spent the night, and she was eager to exchange gifts. She lay there for a moment watching him sleep. Finally, he stirred.

"Wake up, sleepyhead. Merry Christmas," she said.

"Merry Christmas, Bronze." He got out of bed and returned with a large gift-wrapped box.

She was only slightly saddened by the size of the present, wishing instead that he had gotten her something a bit more personal. Bronze loved opening presents. She removed the big, white bow and tore at the green foil paper. Bronze masked her disappointment as she unveiled a pair on tan nubuck boots.

"Do you like them?" he asked.

"Like them? I've only been eyeing them in the window of Lazarus for a month. How'd you know my size?"

"Just a little detective work. You sure you like them, because you can exchange them."

"I love them. Really. Now open your present." He looked at the small, flat, rectangular box and smiled, giving it a little shake before opening it. He pulled out a gold marine link bracelet.

He pecked her lips, cognizant of the fact that he hadn't brushed his teeth yet. "Thank you, honey. I love it. Here, help me put it on."

It cost more than she had wanted to spend, but she made the sacrifice. After all he was worth it.

Bronze had Christmas dinner with her mother. Just the two of them. She brought the boots, still boxed over for Stephanie to see.

"Gorgeous boots. They obviously cost a pretty penny. Do they fit?"

"You know, I was so disappointed that I didn't even try them on." Bronze removed her shoes and slipped into the boots. The left one went on effortlessly, but she was having trouble with the right one. Thinking that maybe she hadn't removed the last wad of tissue paper at the toe, she reached down and pulled out what turned out to be a small square, velvet jewelry box. Unable to contain her excitement, Bronze found herself staring at a pair of princess-cut diamond stud earrings.

"Oh, Ma, look at 'em. Aren't they beautiful? I love 'em. Let me call him right now." She returned to the living room almost as quickly as she had gone. "He's not home. I almost forgot he's having dinner at his aunt's. I'll call him later."

Bronze bought her mother an ivory angora sweater studded with pearls and a bottle of her favorite perfume, while she in turn received a seafoam silk blouse and a set of dishes.

Rose called to speak with two of her favorite people and to wish them a Merry Christmas. Bronze was in such good spirits from the earrings that she hardly noticed the sadness in her mother's eyes as she hung up with her grandmother.

Chapter 22

With near record snowstorms, January and February were two bitterly cold months for the Midwest. Bronze adjusted to the post-holiday slump and sluggish retail sales at Hubert's. Angela, on the other hand, was never busier at *Candor*. Between her search for the story that would give her a second byline and the perfect name for the new magazine, she hadn't the time or the energy for a love interest, which was fine with her. She was tired of giving out free samples and needed a break from the whole scenario.

By the time February 29th rolled around, Angela had submitted what she thought to be the perfect name for the new publication. Apparently management felt the same because at the March 8th general staff meeting it was announced that Angela Sommers had submitted the winning entry. The new magazine for African-American women would be called *Voila!*

As far as Angela was concerned, the best part of winning the contest was the prize—a weekend trip for two to Washington D.C. with airfare and hotel accommodations included. The highlight of the weekend was a special invitation to a gala affair honoring African-American bachelors in their chosen fields.

The wheels in Angela's head were already turning. An article on eligible Black bachelors might just be the ticket for another byline. After all, *Candor*'s audience was more than seventy percent female, and what woman wouldn't want to read about eligible bachelors with the current male shortage?

Angela's first choice for a traveling companion was Bronze, and later that evening she phoned her best friend and filled Bronze in on the particulars.

"I'd love to go," Bronze responded, "but Brandon and I already made plans to go away that weekend."

"Sounds nice. Where to?"

"The Pocono's."

"Oh, you'll love it," Angela said. "Listen, I gotta run, but I'll see you before you leave."

"Okay, lady. Talk to you later."

Brandon was looking forward to the Pocono's. Just nine more days, and he and Bronze would be off on their very first weekender. Lately, Brandon could think of nothing else but Bronze. Sometimes he'd be at the office engrossed in his work, and he'd suddenly remember the softness of her skin or the way her lips curled up when she smiled.

Brandon knew their relationship was at a turning point, and he was torn. On one hand he feared commitment. What if he was just in love with her looks? She certainly was a beauty. On her worst day she looked better than most women at their best. But on the other hand, he knew she was a gem, she was wife material.

He couldn't risk losing her. She meant too much to him. One thing for sure, their weekend would be a barometer of their future together.

Capricia was thrilled to be back in Middle Heights. Not because of the conference that had brought her there, but because she was on a mission to get Brandon back.

She had heard through the grapevine that Brandon was dating some chick that worked at the mall. So the first thing she did was size up the competition. Capricia headed for the Velvet counter as soon as she entered Hubert's. She spotted Bronze right away by the description her sister gave her.

Is *this* my competition? Is this *it*? She suppressed a yawn. This was gonna be a piece of cake! She'd have Brandon back in no time and would see to it that he was thoroughly de-Bronzed. Capricia gave Bronze a good look-over, though there wasn't much to look at as far as she was concerned, then rolled her eyes. But if looks could kill, Bronze would have been dead two minutes earlier.

"Need some help?" Bronze asked innocently with the same welcoming smile she offered to all of her customers.

"Yes. I need some Cherry Red lipstick and nail polish," Capricia said simply. "My boyfriend loves it on me. We're getting back together. He flew me in from Atlanta just to get the ball rolling again. He's been seeing someone else, but he just can't get me outta his mind. You know how *that* is."

"I hope things work out for you both." Bronze

smiled. She returned with Capricia's requested items. "Anything else?"

"No, that'll be all."

Capricia started to pay with cash, but in a split second changed her mind. She wanted Bronze to know exactly who she was. As she handed Bronze her credit card, she could tell that her identity had finally registered.

"Enjoy your day." Capricia smiled, walking away smugly.

Bronze spoke to Brandon later in the week. She didn't mention Capricia's name, and neither did he. The truth was that she hadn't believed a word that Capricia said. But as she sat in the apartment Friday night with her bags packed ready for the Pocono's, doubts began to form.

Brandon was already half an hour late. She sat on the couch wondering what was keeping him. That, at least, was easier than wondering *who* was keeping him. Bronze checked her watch. Fifteen more minutes had already passed.

She decided to give him a call. The phone just rang and rang. The kind of empty ring that said no one is home. He didn't answer his cell phone either. Bronze hung up and peered out her living room window, but there was no sign of Brandon's car.

Finally, Bronze called Angela who was leaving for D.C. later that evening.

"All set for your getaway?" Angela asked.

"He stood me up." Bronze wanted to cry.

"What? What happened?"

"Capricia Moore's in town. He's probably with her right now."

"You don't know that. He's crazy about you," Angela said, wedging the phone between her shoulder and ear to free her hands for packing.

"What's that got to do with it? You know men; they wanna have their cake and eat it too. Boy, I really had him pegged wrong."

"Hey, I got an idea. You're already packed. Why don't you come with me to D.C.?" Angela said.

"I thought your sister was going with you?"

"Oh, you know newlyweds. She'd rather be with her husband."

"Are you sure?"

"Positive. And think of it this way. When he does finally call, he'll know you weren't home sitting by the phone waiting for it to ring. Like my mother always says, 'One monkey don't stop no show.'"

"Angela, I don't even know if I can get a ticket."

"I'll transfer my sister's ticket to your name. Live a little."

"I may as well. It beats sitting here looking out the window," Bronze sighed.

"That's what I'm talking about."

Chapter 23

Four hours later Bronze and Angela's plane touched down at Dulles International Airport. A limousine was waiting to whisk them off to the Embassy Suite in downtown D.C. After unpacking they headed downstairs for something to eat as the plane food had not been to their liking, but then what else could be expected? Unfortunately, the kitchen was already closed, and they were out of luck.

"I know. Let's go to the ice cream shop next door, get something really decadent like a double deluxe chocolate hot fudge sundae, come back to the room, and pig out," Angela suggested. And that's exactly what the two did. They gorged themselves on junk food and collapsed across the beds.

"You know what I'm tempted to do?" Bronze asked without waiting for an answer. "Call Brandon to see if his butt is home."

"And what if he isn't?"

"That's his privilege."

"And what if he is?"

"I'll hang up."

"Hey, do what ya gotta do."

Bronze picked up the phone and dialed Brandon's number before she lost her nerve. Angela could tell by the expression on her face when she hung up that Brandon was still not home.

"Cheer up, Bronze. Just think of all those gorgeous, eligible bachelors we'll be meeting tomorrow." But that was the last thought on Bronze's mind as she drifted off to sleep.

Saturday morning Bronze and Angela slept until around noon. Then they called room service and ordered brunch.

"Let's really glam up for tonight," Angela said. "You never know who we might meet. Imagine an entire room of successful, eligible bachelors. My mouth is watering already."

"Dag," Bronze said fidgeting with her suitcase. "I just broke a nail. Let's see if there's someplace where we can get a manicure."

They strolled into DJ's Unisex Cut and Nail. DJ's was much larger than it appeared from the outside. Nevertheless, Bronze and Angela had to wait more than an hour before getting their nails done. Angela chose a daredevil red polish. She said it matched her mood. She felt racy, bold. She tried to talk Bronze out of a French manicure but to no avail. Bronze felt numb, and she didn't care who knew it.

"Look," Angela told Bronze after they returned to the hotel. "You can be as down and depressed as you wanna be—when you get home. But while we're here, snap out of it. I don't know where Brandon is right now, but I guarantee he's not crying over you. For all you know, you might meet your prince tonight."

"Wouldn't that be something?" Bronze smiled to herself.

"Never can tell," Angela said, grinning at her friend.

What started out as a dull, bourgeois affair turned in to an interesting evening. Twelve eligible African-American bachelors were honored by the American Media Association for their contributions in various fields ranging from law and sports to politics and business. After the awards had been presented and dinner served, the best part of the evening for Angela—the mingling hour began.

It didn't take Angela all day to figure out with whom she wanted to rub shoulders, she cut her eyes straight to NBA hoop star Clive Dixon. All those nights in front of the television lusting after Clive with his sweaty, glistening, golden body didn't prepare her for their chance meeting.

Damn he looks good, she almost said out loud as she gave him the once-over. From the table where she and Bronze were seated with several other reporters, she had a relatively good view of Clive, but it couldn't possibly compare with the view she intended on having as she made her way across the room toward him.

He was being interviewed by Renee Reeves, a reporter from *Style* magazine, and when she made her exit, Angela moved in.

"Hi, Clive," she said, extending her hand. "I'm Angela Sommers from *Candor* magazine.

"Oh, please. Not another interview," he said good naturedly.

"On one condition." She smiled up at the six-foot-seven-inch frame.

"What's that?"

"An autograph."

"Consider it done," he said, signing her program.

Back at the table Bronze relived the twist of events that had brought her to D.C., not bothering to make small talk with the others at her table. Brandon had just broken the last G—treat me good. He turned out to be a dog like all the rest. He was probably with Capricia at that very moment. The bum. Damn him.

Bronze got up from the table and headed for the ladies' lounge, fishing in her purse for a tissue and not really looking where she was going. That's when she walked smack-dab into honoree Councilman Adam Malone and his cocktail. The drink spilled all over her dress, and the councilman could not apologize enough. Bronze was close to tears and Malone offered to pay for the cleaning of her dress.

"Just send me the bill, and I'll take care of it," he promised. He gave her his handkerchief to wipe her tears. "You're too pretty to be crying. It can't be that bad. What's wrong?"

Bronze hesitated for a moment. He sounded genuinely concerned. She looked up at him. He was tall with broad shoulders that were probably good for crying on. Just beginning to gray at the temples, the councilman had a slight moustache. He had that big man on campus look. He was regal. Like a prince. She smiled remembering what Angela had said.

"Well, something just put a smile on your face. Does that smile come with a name?"

"I'm Bronze," she said.

"Nice to meet you. I'm Councilman Adam Malone," he said, extending his hand.

"Yes, I know. You're running for Congress in Atlanta." They shook hands.

He grinned. "Let's sit down," he said, guiding her to an empty table.

Normally not one to warm up quickly to strange men, Bronze was surprised at how at ease she felt with the councilman.

"You don't strike me as a reporter."

"I'm not. My girlfriend's with *Candor* magazine."

"So what's got you so down, Bronze?" he asked.

Suddenly, Bronze found herself telling this stranger everything from the way she and Brandon met, to her suspicions about him being with Capricia at that very moment.

"You know, Bronze, let me share with you something I've learned about life. Things may seem hopeless now, but cheer up. There's always tomorrow. So why think the worst before you have to? Let him screw up first before you write him off. Give him a chance. Life is so unpredictable. Have you ever seen that old Cary Grant movie, *An Affair to Remember?* Anything could have happened. A man would have to be nuts to let you slip through his fingers."

"Thanks, but you hardly know me."

"True. But I'm in politics, and over the years you learn how to judge character. It's a fine art. Not only are you gorgeous, you're bright, sensitive, and a real lady. Your parents must be very proud of you."

"Yes," she said simply.

"And they've done a fantastic job of raising you." Malone checked his watch. "Well, Bronze, it was a pleasure meeting you. I'm afraid I have to run. Here, take my card. I'll be expecting your dry cleaning bill," he said, rising.

"Take care," Bronze said, watching him go and wondering why she had just divulged her personal life to a total stranger.

Chapter 24

Bronze returned home on a rainy Sunday afternoon and was bombarded with messages on her answering machine from Brandon. She was in no rush whatsoever to return his calls. In fact, she kept her machine on and screened her calls accordingly. Brandon called once again, and finally she picked up the phone.

"I've been trying to get you all weekend. Where the hell have you been?" Brandon asked.

"Where the hell have I been? Where the hell have you been?"

"Look, we need to talk. I'll be right over."

"Suit yourself," she snapped and hung up.

Twenty minutes later he arrived, bloodshot eyes and all, to explain. His cousin had called him hysterical from the hospital half an hour before he was due to pick up Bronze.

"Well, you should have just called his parents."

"Remember I told you I had a cousin who worked for Velvet?"

"Oh, it was her? What happened?"

"It's not a she. It's a he."

Suddenly Bronze got a sick feeling in the pit of her stomach. "Wait a minute. You don't mean Julian Mitchell?"

"Yeah. Julian's my cousin. You know him?"

"We met at a Velvet workshop. What happened?"

"Let's just say he came between some gay bashers and a bottle of malt liquor."

"Oh my God, no." She sat down on the couch, not trusting her knees to support her.

"He didn't want the rest of the family to know so he called me."

"How is he?"

"Hurtin'. The hospital kept him overnight, but he's home now with bruised ribs and nine stitches across his forehead. I'm really sorry about this weekend, but it couldn't be helped."

"Shhhh." She put her arms around him, and they embraced. "It's okay. I understand."

He hugged Bronze tighter and began kissing her neck and cheeks. Finally, he kissed her lips gently like a precious possession, then deeply. His tongue searched her mouth and the heat rose in their bodies. His touch felt so good.

Bronze led him to the bedroom, and they quickly undressed in the darkness before falling back onto the bed. Brandon's mouth found her nipples, and she rubbed his strong, hard back. She let out a moan as he touched her moistness with his fingers.

He started to enter her, but she told him she wasn't ready yet. So, he waited until neither of them could stand it any longer. He spread her lips and entered her wetness. She wrapped her legs around him, and he went in deeper. It was so good. He was hitting just the right spot. She let out another moan as she came. Finally, Brandon's breathing became hard and loud, and she knew that he had cum too.

Catching their breath, they lay back on the bed. As Brandon dozed off, Bronze looked over at him. Just a few minutes ago he had been all over her, and now he lay exhausted and defenseless. Bronze was tempted to awaken him, but Brandon once told her that if she was awake, she expected the entire household to be awake too. He was such a beautiful man. She smiled. She loved his body from those long, sexy eyelashes to his hands, which always made her feel so wonderful.

Her thoughts drifted to Julian. Months ago she couldn't get enough of him. She had wanted him that much. Now she felt a numbness at the mention of his name. Time had a way of lessening pain. She was truly sorry about the attack. He didn't deserve that kind of treatment. No human being did. She silently prayed for his recovery. What were the odds that she and Julian's cousin would end up together? She could never tell Brandon about her relationship with Julian. Somehow, Bronze didn't think Brandon would understand. Hopefully, Julian would keep their involvement a secret too. Some things were better left unsaid.

Again Bronze watched Brandon sleep. He always made her feel so sexy. But more than that she was in love with him, though neither of them ever mentioned the L word.

Perhaps sensing her absorption, he stirred and opened his eyes. "A penny for your thoughts?" Brandon said simply.

"A penny? These thoughts are worth at least a quarter." She smiled.

He reached for his pants and came up with sixteen cents. "How about an IOU?" he asked as he threw his jeans back on the floor. "I'm good for it."

"I'm sure you are, but with me it's all or nothing."

"Then do me a favor. Hold on to those thoughts until I'm worthy of them," he said seriously.

"Deal," she said, shaking his outstretched hand. Only she wasn't so sure that he hadn't already read her mind.

Brandon rolled over and reached for Bronze, as the raindrops danced on the windowpane.

Chapter 25

Stephanie sat down to read the morning paper over a cup a coffee just as the telephone rang. She checked the clock over the kitchen sink. Who'd be calling at this hour? Only one person.

"Hi, Bronze."

"How'd you know it was me?"

"Mother's intuition. Your grandmother called last night. Vanessa had the baby. A little girl. She named her Amber Rose, after your grandmother."

"Oh, that's wonderful. How are they?"

"They're both fine."

"Was she in labor long?"

"No, your grandmother said they barely made it to the hospital."

"I guess Amber wanted out." Bronze laughed and her mother joined in.

"We'll have to go see them one weekend."

"Absolutely," Stephanie agreed. "So, what's been happening with you?"

Bronze told her mother about her weekend from

Brandon's call, which never came, to the dinner in D.C. and finally to Julian's and Brandon's family ties.

"Imagine Brandon and Julian being cousins. Jasmine was right after all. Can you believe it? Small world, isn't it?"

"Smaller than you know," Stephanie agreed.

"I don't think I'll tell Brandon about Julian and me. At least not yet. I don't think he'd understand. You know how territorial men can be."

"Well, just be careful your decision doesn't backfire in your face."

Bronze changed the subject. "You know I met one of the honorees at the D.C. event, Councilman Malone." Stephanie didn't bat an eye. "And Ma, I'm telling you he'd be perfect for you."

"Uh-oh, here we go again. My daughter the matchmaker."

"I'm serious, Ma. He's just your type."

"And what exactly is my type?"

"He's well-spoken, intelligent, charming, refined, and real easy on the eyes. There's gotta be a way of getting you two together; I'll be working on it. Have you read Paige Lawson's column yet?"

"No. I just picked up the paper."

"Let me read it to you," Bronze said. "Councilman Adam Malone, one of Atlanta's finest bachelors, is tossing his hat in the ring for Congressman against the incumbent Robert Carson. The consensus at the Carson camp is that if Malone is as slick with his political endeavors as he is with the ladies, Carson's time is just about up. We'll just have to stay tuned, won't we?"

"And you're trying to get me involved with this skirt-chasing rascal? No thank you."

"Ma, you can't believe everything you hear. She's trying to sell papers. And besides, I met the man in person. Remember?"

"Enough about him," Stephanie said.

"What's on your agenda tonight?" Bronze asked.

"Leo, who else?" Stephanie sighed.

Leo Stone hadn't swept Stephanie off her feet, but at least she could depend on him for a night out when the mood struck her. And there were no strings attached. He was attentive and dependable.

"But, Ma, if he bores you that much, why are you still with him? You need some excitement. Someone who can get those juices flowing and put the sparkle back in your eyes."

"Bronze, one day you will learn that it's more important to be loved than to be in love."

"Not in my book. Like the poet said, 'If equal affection cannot be, let the more loving one be me.' Why can't we have it both ways?"

"Because life isn't always fair. So you must decide what price you're willing to pay. Don't ever forget that, Bronze."

At Congressman Robert Carson's campaign headquarters, Councilman Malone was the topic of conversation. The congressman was the least pleased with the results of the poll taken two days ago, which showed that forty-two percent of the constituents in Atlanta's sixteenth congressional district would vote for the councilman if the election were held that day. They cited the need for a fresh approach in dealing with the town's problems. The incumbent was particularly dismayed with the plunge in his own approval rating since Councilman Malone's announcement to run against him last month.

Politricks was a dirty game, and Robert Carson's motto was "whatever works." He was quite the pragmatist, which was how he had been elected to an unprecedented fourth term, and how he intended to win his fifth.

He called one of his campaign advisors into his office. A.T. Winters cared more about being associated with a winner than anything else, which was why he was not at all surprised by his boss's remarks.

"Look, I want you to find the skeletons in Malone's closet. I don't care what it takes or who it takes, but you better find something or come Election Day, we'll both be sitting on our butts collecting unemployment."

"I'll get right on it, Robert," Winters said.

Chapter 26

Stephanie curled up on the sofa with two old friends—a good book and a mug of hot herbal tea. It was one of those days when she felt like doing nothing. She soon realized that she had read the same page twice. She couldn't concentrate. Her mind was elsewhere.

Leo Stone was a dear, sweet man, but she didn't love him although she had tried. And one shouldn't have to try. Not where love was concerned. Her attitude was changing. Maybe being loved wasn't always more important than loving.

He and Stephanie enjoyed each other's company for the most part, but there were times when she found him dull. Leo was so predictable. There was no spontaneity. Not even in bed.

She'd been thinking a lot lately about taking a cruise or flying down to the Islands, something that would freshen her perspective. Maybe Bronze was right. She needed excitement in her life. Someone who could get those juices flowing again. She was still young.

Her mind drifted to yesteryear. To a happier relationship. A time when she had dove eagerly into the pool of love and nearly drowned. Stephanie didn't often allow herself to think of him. Becoming a prisoner of her past, trapped in another lifetime was much too easy. She experienced spasms of anguish and despair upon returning to that part of her heart. The part she kept locked away. As the memories flooded her consciousness, she felt excruciating pain and shame. She remembered Bronze's father and the love they shared. Hot tears welled up in her eyes and spilled down her cheeks. She let them flow. Stephanie needed a good cry. Their relationship had been bittersweet. Like life.

Angela sat in Ebony's opposite her date for the evening, bored to pieces. She sized him up. Don Baker was as exciting as iceberg lettuce with his side part and straight-laced polyester clothes. Was he for real? She was tired of making stabs at conversation with him when his only response was an occasional grunt. She had promised herself that she'd never let her sister, Dee, fix her up again after that fiasco with Keith at the Christmas party.

It had gotten to the point where Angela was actually counting the number of sprinklers on the ceiling. Maybe Don wasn't a total loser. It was just that she could have thought of a million other things she'd rather be doing at that moment than spending time with him, like cleaning her oven or rearranging her closets.

She was getting antsy sitting there bouncing to the music and making eye contact with a brother by the bar. Angela was tempted to walk up to him and order him a drink, but that was a little risqué even for her.

Just my luck, she thought. *A gorgeous, corn bread-fed buck is checking me out, and I'm stuck here with chopped liver.*

Just then Don made his best move of the entire evening as far as Angela was concerned. He went to the men's room. She glanced over at the buck on the bar stool, and their eyes locked. *Make that move,* she thought, willing him with her mind. Finally, he was standing by her.

"I couldn't help but notice you from across the room. Was that your boyfriend?" he asked.

"Would you believe a blind date?" Angela answered, thankful that she was not all glammed up and reeking of high expectations for the evening.

"Say no more." He smiled.

Shit. Don was on his way back to the table. She thought fast. "Don, this is an old classmate from junior high." She almost said junior lie rather than high. "Meet umh, umh . . ."

"Drew," he said, catching on quickly to her game.

"Right," she said. "Do you ever see what's her name?" she asked, snapping her fingers as if trying to recall a name.

"Oh, you mean Glenda? She and Todd got married last year."

"You're kidding? That's great."

"I don't see a ring on your finger. Still single?"

"You know me, Drew. I'm just waiting for the right one. Angela's in no rush. Know what I mean?"

"Damn straight, Angela. Listen, here's my number. Give me a call, and maybe we can all hook up and talk about old times."

"Sounds good. I'll be in touch, Drew," she said, taking his card.

"I hope so." He winked, exiting just as smoothly as he had approached her. The entire conversation went over Don's head.

Bronze ushered in spring with pep in her step. Winter was gone along with the snowstorms and the darkness associated with it. Yes, bleakness succumbed to the splendor of new life. Things were going well between Brandon and herself, and she had just gotten another raise at work.

Bronze was looking forward to lunching with Stephanie, who had just returned from the Virgin Islands over the Easter break. Tanned and rested, Stephanie was pleased to be in the company of her favorite person.

"So what's new, kiddo?"

"You are, Ma," Bronze answered. "Look at you. You look terrific. This vacation definitely agreed with you."

"Well, I did a lot of soul searching on the beach, and I came to the conclusion that you were right. I'm not rocking-chair material yet, and I do need some excitement in my life. Unfortunately, Leo doesn't fit the bill."

"Have you spoken to him since you've been back?"

"As a matter of fact we had dinner last night, and I broke the news to him gently. He's a wonderful catch for someone, but I'm just not that someone. We'll always be friends."

"I'm glad you're still friends."

"So how's Brandon?"

"Oh, he's fine. He's been a real sweetheart lately."

"You know what your grandmother says: 'You hooked 'im, now reel 'im in.' "

They finished their lunch and topped it off with

cheesecake. Stephanie picked up the tab. "This one's on me," she said.

Three weeks later Stephanie began dating Ross Pinkston, her part-time tennis instructor. From her very first lesson, Stephanie sensed a mutual attraction. Since he was also an educator, they had much in common. She couldn't remember the last time she'd felt that way about a man. Especially a white man. One evening after her lesson he invited Stephanie out for drinks.

"So tell me about yourself, Stephanie."

"Why do I get the feeling I'm being interviewed?" Stephanie asked, smiling.

"Maybe you are."

"For what position might that be?"

"Which one would you like?" Ross nonchalantly replied.

"I'll leave that alone." She shook her head, amused.

"For now anyway."

"You sound awfully sure of yourself," Stephanie said.

"Of us, you mean. I'm sure of us. But tell me if I'm wrong," he said staring deeply into her eyes. Stephanie was the first to look away. She traced the rim of her wineglass with her fingertip and looked up.

Ross was deeply tanned with hazel eyes and dark brown hair. She wondered what it would be like to be with him. Then she pushed the thought aside. After all, she wasn't a teenager, and it took more than sex to make a relationship work. They finished the rest of their drinks and centered the conversation around safer topics like the bestsellers list, since they were both avid readers and, of course, the game where love meant nothing more than who might win a tennis match.

A.T. Winters had been running background checks on Councilman Malone, and so far the councilman was as clean as a whistle. Which only meant one thing. He'd just have to dig deeper.

Let's see, he thought. Malone was born and bred in Dawnville, Ohio, and moved to Atlanta when he was twenty-four years old. That was all in the public bio. Maybe it would be worth his while to take a trip to this Dawnville and check things out.

He called Robert Carson to discuss his next move and then made plane reservations. Dawnville was so small that there was no airport. He'd have to fly into Columbus and from there, rent a car and drive into Dawnville.

He'd be in one of those hick towns all right. He wasn't really looking forward to that. But then again, maybe that would be to his advantage. Everybody knew that little towns were dens of lust and torrid affairs.

Chapter 27

Winters spent less than a day in Dawnville, Ohio before he'd kicked up something that he thought to be strong enough to bring the councilman down. His first stop was the public library where he scanned old editions of *Dawnville Times* on microfiche. His search began with the year of Councilman Malone's birth.

Winters noted the usual high school extra-curricular and scholastic events such as basketball MVP, captain of the debate team, and prom king. It seemed as though Malone was a big man on campus. Winters knew the type. He was probably the kind of son of which his own father would have been proud. From day one, Alfred Tyler Winters had been a disappointment. He thought for a moment, and a smile crept up on his face revealing dingy, crooked teeth. It would be a real pleasure destroying Malone. Yes, indeed. A real pleasure.

Tired eyes and all, he continued his search through the newspaper. And then he noticed a small two-by-two-inch article that immediately had him headed for the librarian's desk. A tiny, persistent alarm went off in his head. Winters knew he was on to something.

He approached the elderly librarian with her golden-framed bifocals and her prim silver bun. Her eyebrows looked like McDonald's arches. And from the looks of her pink frosted lipstick, she never learned how to color within the lines. Of course she wasn't married. At least her nameplate didn't betray her spinsterhood. Winters quickly glanced at her feet. Yep, those orthopedic jobs. One thing for sure, she'd never catch a husband in those shoes.

"Excuse me, Miss Jones, where's the courthouse?" he asked.

"You must be new in these parts. Everyone knows the county courthouse is over in Evanston."

"Actually, I'm a reporter from *Tempo* magazine, and I'm doing research on Councilman Malone. Know anything about him?"

"Ever since he decided to run for Congress, this place has been swarming with nosy outsiders like you," she reprimanded.

Winters left shaking his head. Either those shoes were pinching her bunions or she hadn't had a piece in a long while. Either way she was a crab.

Winters got into his rented Oldsmobile and pulled out a map of North Central Ohio. The Evanston County courthouse was only twenty miles away, but somehow Winters managed to get lost. He felt like such a wimp as he pulled into a BP gas station. 'Can't you do anything right?' he heard his father ask him.

A man came out in worn overalls bearing a faded name patch that read *Smitty.*

"Hey, I'm looking for the Evanston County courthouse. Can you help me?" Winters asked.

"Stay on this road here, and make a left at the first light. Then go down about five blocks, and you'll see a

Hardee's on the corner. Make a sharp right, and that'll put you on Cedar Parkway. Stay on the parkway for about fifteen minutes until you get to the North Main Street exit. And that'll take you straight to the courthouse. It's on the right. You can't miss it."

"Thanks a lot."

"You a lawyer?" Smitty asked.

"No, a reporter. Know anything about Councilman Malone?"

"Isn't he running for something in Atlanta?"

"That's the one. Know anything about him?" Winters repeated.

"All depends. How much is it worth to you?" Smitty stuffed his hands into the pockets of his overalls and rocked back on his heels.

Winters pulled out a fifty.

"That's chicken shit, mister. And I don't gossip." Winters added another twenty to the ante. At which point Smitty yawned. "Don't waste my time. I don't open my mouth for anything less than two hundred."

"A hundred."

"One fifty," Smitty insisted.

"Deal."

Four hours later Congressman Robert Carson received a phone call from Winters before he boarded the plane back to Atlanta.

"So what's the word?" Carson asked simply.

"Oh, it's on. It's definitely on! Let's just say the councilman's double-dipping past is about to catch up with him."

* * *

It had been a long day for Councilman Adam Malone. First a harrowing meeting with the city council on the proposed budget cuts, and then a fund-raising dinner later that evening sponsored by Atlanta's Black Democratic Coalition. As he took a hot shower and prepared for bed, he had no idea of how drained he was until his head hit the pillow. He was out in no time.

It wasn't until after the phone rang that Adam realized he had forgotten to turn on his answering machine as he normally did at night.

"Hello?"

"Malone?"

"Yes."

"Eight six seven six."

"Who the hell is this?"

"Don't worry about it."

"Oh, you just want me to hit the lottery. Go to hell." And with that he hung up. Two seconds later the phone rang again, but Adam was in no mood for pranks. He finally took the phone off the hook and drifted off to sleep. He dreamed about winning the lottery.

Adam was up before dawn preparing his speech to the senior citizen's board for that night. The phone rang for the umpteenth time.

It was the anonymous caller from the night before. "Eight six seven six." And then he hung up.

Adam removed his glasses, stood, and stretched. He had written the numbers down after the first call. Yet, he was unable to pinpoint their significance. He let out a sigh and returned to his speech. There was much to be done before the election.

Chapter 28

Bronze drove Brandon's car to drop him off at the airport. He would only be gone a week for job training in Atlanta, but she couldn't help but worry about him. After all, he would be in Capricia's territory, and no matter how long his training lasted during the day, there were always the nights. And Brandon would be gone for six nights. Six long nights. It wasn't that she didn't trust Brandon, but she refused to underestimate Capricia.

They said good-bye at the curb. "Be good," she wanted to add, but didn't. As she searched his eyes, she wondered if he could read her thoughts.

Two hours later Brandon boarded the plan with ambivalence. He knew that though he had just left Bronze's loving arms, he would be welcomed into Capricia's outstretched ones just a few hours later if that's what he wanted. It was tempting. All men craved a woman in every port. At least if they were honest with themselves. It was a male fantasy. And Brandon was no angel. As a matter of fact, his frat brothers had nicknamed him The Juggler.

Once Brandon settled into his hotel room he debated whether or not to call Capricia. She didn't even know that he was in town, and he almost preferred it that way. Almost, but not quite. It wasn't until Wednesday evening after class that his resolve weakened.

He picked up the phone and dialed her number. He hated talking to her answering machine, so he left a brief message.

Two hours later Brandon found himself in Capricia's company. She had returned his call and invited him over.

"So, Brandon, how long have you been in town?" Capricia asked after dinner.

"Since Saturday."

"And you're just calling me now? Who are you afraid of? Yourself or us?"

Brandon took a good, long look at Capricia. He had to admit she still had it going on.

As if sensing his apprehension, Capricia moved closer to him on the couch. "You know when you called me this evening you made my day, Brandon."

"I can't promise you. . . ."

"Shhh," she interrupted, kissing him deeply. "Don't talk. Let's just enjoy tonight."

During the entire plane ride home Brandon could not get her out of his mind. He remembered everything—her scent, her laughter, her smile. He could no longer deny his feelings, and the trip to Atlanta clinched it. He thought long and hard. Finally he realized what he would do.

One day after work Brandon stopped at Miller's Jewelers. He was about to make a special purchase. It was time to buy *the* ring. The saleswoman just happened to be a friend of Capricia's sister, and she helped Brandon pick out a one-carat engagement ring. He hoped that she would keep it under wraps, but by the knowing smile she gave him, somehow he doubted it.

A couple of days later Yvette Moore finally caught up with her sister Capricia at Congressman Carson's office. "I've been trying to get you for two days. Where have you been?"

"Uncle Rob has been working us like crazy around here lately. You know it's an election year. What's up?" As much as Yvette hated it, Capricia had to put her on speaker phone, frantically attempting to complete an envelope stuffing task.

"Well, little sister, looks like you're gonna beat me to the altar."

"What are you talking about?"

"You know Kelly works at Miller's Jewelers, right?" Yvette asked.

"Yeah."

"She just sold Brandon an engagement ring." At that, Capricia snatched the receiver from its cradle. Those damn envelopes could wait.

"Get outta here." Her eyes popped open as a smile took over the entire bottom half of her face.

"I'm serious. No joke. And you know Kelly. Girlfriend tried to sell him the biggest rock in the store. Whatever you did to him on his trip worked."

"Let's just say I showed him a *real* good time. Nothing wrong with a little Southern hospitality." They both laughed.

Capricia hung up feeling absolutely ecstatic. She hugged herself as she swiveled around in her chair. Now if she could only contain herself until he proposed.

Brandon called Bronze. He had to see her; they had to talk. He picked her up and drove out to the lake. Bronze noticed that Brandon was very quiet. All during the ride he kept his eyes on the road and hardly said a word. She wondered what the silence was about and tried not to jump to conclusions.

He parked the car and turned to face her. "Bronze we've had some beautiful times together. I've loved being with you these past months. You're a special person, and any man would be lucky to have you in his life." He paused briefly. "Something happened to me in Atlanta. I can't explain it."

An alarm went off in Bronze's head. *Oh God, he's dumping me for Capricia. They're getting back together. I knew it.* "Brandon, wait please don't."

"Let me finish." He was starting to sweat. "I love you, Bronze." He took the velvet ring box from his pocket and opened it up to reveal what Bronze thought was the most exquisite marquise-and-baguette diamond ring. "Will you marry me?"

She looked at Brandon and then back to the ring while her mouth dropped wide open. She threw her arms around his neck and squeezed him so hard that he almost dropped the ring box.

"Is that a yes?"

All she could do was nod. As he slid the ring on her finger, her eyes welled with tears. Happy tears. She didn't trust herself to speak. Bronze Sutton and Brandon Wilde were getting married.

It was well after midnight when the sound of the telephone broke Stephanie's sleep. "Hello?" she said groggily.

"Ma, guess what?" She didn't wait for an answer. "I'm engaged! Brandon just proposed. Can you believe it?"

Stephanie was now wide awake. "Oh sweetheart, that's wonderful. I'm so happy for you."

"And, Ma, you gotta see this ring!"

"A real knockout, huh?"

"You got it."

"Have you guys set a date?"

"No, but we don't want a long engagement."

"Your grandmother will be thrilled. You know how much she adores Brandon."

"I still can't believe it." Bronze talked her mother's ears off for another half hour before she retired to bed. But all through the night she'd wake up and feel for her ring, just to make certain that she wasn't dreaming.

It didn't take long for the news to spread from Middle Heights to Atlanta. Of course, Capricia was pissed to the nth degree. She was utterly infuriated and let Brandon know when she called him days later. In closing, her words to him were, "Just remember this, Brandon. Payback's a bitch."

* * *

At first Stephanie thought there was a problem with her phone. She would answer it, and there'd be dead silence on the other end. She called the phone company and had the line checked. They assured her that everything was fine, but the problem continued. When she realized that her telephone rang every day at the same time, she began to sense that it was more than just a childish prank.

One evening after work, Bronze stopped by her mother's. They were in the kitchen talking, and the telephone rang. Stephanie glanced at the clock. It was 7:30.

Stephanie answered the phone as normally as possible. "Hello?"

"I've got my eye on you."

Stephanie turned her back to Bronze. She didn't recognize the man's voice. She hadn't a clue. The phone went dead. She quietly replaced the phone, not wanting to startle Bronze.

"Ma, who was that?" Bronze asked, rising from the kitchen table.

"Nobody, honey. Just a telemarketer."

The following week Stephanie had her phone number changed to an unlisted one. The threatening phone calls stopped, and Stephanie started to relax. Her life got back to normal.

* * *

"Girlfriend, we have to go out and celebrate. And just think, I'm the one who introduced you two." Angela was thrilled about Bronze's engagement.

They decided on their usual hangout, Ebony's. "It's my treat," Angela said as they grabbed a table. "And let me see that ring again. It's beautiful. I bet Brandon'll be eating out of cans for the rest of the year, poor thing. When's the big day?"

"I don't know. I haven't even met his parents yet. Brandon wants us to drive up to Michigan for his family reunion. I pray Julian doesn't go. Isn't that awful? And I'm nervous about meeting his folks."

"I can understand your issues with Julian. But why are you afraid to meet his parents?"

"What if they don't like me?"

"Puhleez, Bronze. You're a lady. They'll love you. As long as you're good to and for their son, that's all they want. Trust me. Just be yourself. So tell me how Brandon proposed."

Bronze told Angela all about their drive to the lake, including the awful feeling she had at the pit of her stomach all the while, as well as her shock at his proposal. "All I could think of was him and Capricia shacked up in some cozy love nest, and then out of nowhere he pops the question."

"Well, it looks like you've won. Capricia's got nothing on you."

"Nope, nothing but memories."

Just when Stephanie began to relax, the phone calls returned. Apparently, she had been lulled into a false sense of security, because changing her phone number had not solved the problem. It was the same deep voice that churned her stomach. "I've got my eye on you." She slammed the phone down.

Hours later she saw Ross Pinkston. Their relationship was no longer limited to drinks after Stephanie's tennis lessons. They ended up missing their eight o'clock dinner reservations at the Black Thai Restaurant because Stephanie could not pull herself together after that disturbing phone call.

"You look lighter than me in the winter," he said. "What's wrong?"

"Oh, I just had a bad day is all," she said, shaking her head. "But I'm fine now."

"I'll take a rain check if you're not up to it."

"Would you mind terribly?"

"I won't lie and say I wasn't looking forward to dining with you tonight, but I understand. Really." He kissed her on the forehead.

"I have an idea. Why don't we eat in? It'll be fun."

"Are you sure you're up to it?"

"I'd love to have you for dinner, I mean."

"Of course you would." He winked.

They both smiled as Stephanie went to slip into something more comfortable.

Chapter 29

Friday evening Bronze and Brandon drove up to Michigan to meet his family. He was quite proud of his fiancée and thrilled to be finally introducing her to his parents.

Lee and Jean Wilde took an instant liking to their prospective daughter-in-law. However, Brandon's sister, Ashley, was not impressed. In fact, Bronze felt the iciness of her stare almost immediately.

"If Ashley had her way, I'd still be with Capricia. They're old friends from the University of Michigan. Don't worry about Ashley. She'll get over it." Bronze and Brandon carried their luggage into the house. "Hey, she has no choice." Brandon gave Bronze a quick kiss.

Bronze sensed that Ashley was not thrilled to be sharing a room with her. In fact, she made every attempt to discourage any type of small talk between the two of them.

* * *

Brandon lay in his old room thinking about Bronze. He considered smuggling her into his bed, but dared not. He respected his parents too much for that, but the idea was tempting nonetheless. He hoped that Ashley wasn't giving Bronze too hard a way to go. She could be such a bitch when she wanted to.

After days of thunderstorms the weather cooperated on Saturday for the Wilde family reunion held at the Teekawee State Park. There were clear blue skies with plenty of sun.

Bronze met relatives galore, and except for Ashley, they all made her feel welcome and at home. It was obvious to her that Brandon was a favorite, and as she looked up, she saw him holding court with his cousins.

As Bronze sat eating a burger fresh off the grill and making small talk with one of Brandon's cousins, Jean Wilde came over and introduced her to some new arrivals.

"This is Brandon's fiancée, Bronze. And Bronze, this is my sister Olivia and her husband Jim."

"Nice to meet you both," Bronze said. Brandon walked over to them.

"Brandon, that's an exquisite engagement ring, but I hope the two of you don't mind eating bread and water your first year," his aunt said.

"We'll live off love," Brandon joked.

"Hell, when those bills start rolling in, that love goes out the window. Trust me. But you're a lucky man, Brandon. I wish you could talk your cousin Julian into settling down," Uncle Jim said. Bronze almost choked on her burger.

"I'll see what I can do, Uncle Jim," Brandon promised as Jim and Olivia headed toward the grill. "You know, that's my cousin Julian's parents."

"Oh," Bronze said simply. As she and Brandon headed towards the bar, all she could think was that she needed a drink.

The rest of the day was spent chowing down on good food, playing volleyball, and of course, dealing game after game of bid whist. The Wilde clan took plenty of pictures, but the one Brandon treasured most was of him and Bronze.

Bronze could not deny her mother the pleasure of throwing an engagement party two weeks after she and Brandon returned from Michigan. Friends and family gathered to wish them well. Brandon's parents came down from Michigan and met Stephanie for the first time. Brandon's sister, Ashley, did not attend. Rose Sutton wouldn't have missed it for the world—arthritis or not.

"Mrs. Sutton, it's good seeing you again," Brandon said.

"You can call me Grandma. We're practically family." Rose patted his hand. She was quite fond of her granddaughter's fiancé.

Vanessa and Dave came with the baby. It was the first time Bronze and Stephanie had seen the newest addition to the family. Like most one-month old babies, Amber did little more than eat and sleep. She was oblivious to all the laughter and chatter around her, lying contently in her father's arms.

Bronze looked at the two of them sitting on the sofa. It seemed to be a perfect Kodak moment. Whenever she saw a father devoted to his daughter, a feeling washed over her that she could not explain. It was a strange mixture of longing, anger, and sadness. She wished that things could have been different in her life, but she had made it all these years without him.

Brandon approached her from behind. “Promise me that we’ll have plenty of those,” he said, referring to Amber.

“Absolutely, Mr. Wilde,” Bronze said, turning and looking into his eyes. Then the sadness passed. She had so much to look forward to that she didn’t want to look back.

Angela didn’t mind telling everyone that she was responsible for Bronze and Brandon’s pending nuptials. In fact, when someone mentioned how lucrative the matchmaking industry had become, Angela made a mental note for a future *Candor* article.

Everyone wanted to know if Brandon and Bronze had set a date. “No, not yet, but we’re working on it,” Bronze admitted.

“Well, may the road always rise up to meet you, and may the wind always be at your back,” Rose said.

“Here, here,” everyone agreed as they toasted the happy couple.

Chapter 30

During the next few weeks, Bronze began pouring over bridal magazines in preparation for her wedding day. She and Brandon were constantly surfing the web for the best deals at local reception halls. Neither realized just how expensive the packages could be. They decided on a budget and requested videos of all the reception halls that fell within it.

One Friday evening after work, Bronze invited Brandon over to look at the videos that had come in during that week. They both liked the first two videos, but disliked the third. Bronze loved the fourth, while Brandon thought it left much to be desired. He preferred the fifth over the second and was having second thoughts about the first.

"I thought we agreed that we both liked the first two," Bronze said.

"But that was before I saw the fifth one," he admitted. "Look, if it'll make you happy, I'll go with your choice."

"Just like that?"

"All I want is you. As long as you're there, nothing

else matters. We can have the reception at the bowling alley for all I care."

"Nice try, but we still have four more videos to watch," she reminded him.

"All right, you win. Let me go get some more popcorn and stuff, and I'll be set."

Bronze rewound the tape as Brandon returned with snacks and another beer. She inserted the next video into her VCR and they got comfortable on the sofa.

A woman wearing a robe appeared on the screen. She eased back onto the bed. Her mate removed her robe revealing nothing underneath. He climbed on top of her, and they began to make love. Suddenly, the focus changed and their faces appeared. It was Brandon and Capricia. He wore nothing but the gold bracelet she had bought him for Christmas.

"You son of a bitch!" Bronze spewed out as she jumped up. "Get out!"

"Wait, I can explain." The color had left his face, leaving him almost white.

"I want you out of here, now!" She quickly removed her engagement ring and flung it at him. Surprisingly, he caught it. "Get out," she screamed at the top of her lungs as the tears chased each other down her cheeks. She was devastated.

Like a dog with his tail between its legs, Brandon quietly left her apartment. Bronze waited until he drove off before collapsing on the couch.

The moment Brandon had left Bronze's apartment after viewing the videotape, he had rushed home to call Capricia. He hadn't cared how late it was. If he woke that bitch up, so be it.

She had answered on the third ring, her voice groggy with sleep. "Hello?"

"What the hell do you mean taping us?"

"Oh hi, Brandon. I've been expecting your call. How's that fiancée of yours? On her way to becoming a blushing bride, no doubt."

"You'll pay for this, bitch!"

"Pay for what? Don't tell me the wedding is off? Didn't she enjoy my gift? Maybe we can make another one. I'm game if you are."

"Go to hell!" He hung up angrier than ever.

The next couple of weeks were hell for Bronze as she simply went through the motions of living. She took a few days off from work and refused to accept any phone calls, except from her mother. While at home bingeing on butter-pecan ice cream, chocolate chip cookies, and other comfort foods, her doorbell rang. It was the florist. Brandon had sent her a dozen roses, begging her forgiveness, but she refused to accept his guilt-ridden bouquet. She promptly told the deliveryman to return them. Brandon began leaving hourly messages on her voice mail to no avail. Irritated by the mere sound of his voice, she finally called the phone company and changed her number to an unlisted one, and blocked his number from her cell.

Bronze called Angela to fill her in on the latest and to give her, her new phone number. She made her promise not to give it to Brandon.

"Of course not," Angela agreed. "But you should see him, Bronze. The man looks like he's lost his best friend."

"Well as far as I'm concerned, he has. I feel like I'm trapped in a nightmare. I keep hoping my alarm clock will go off, and I'll wake up and realize this has all been just a bad dream."

"I know, sweetie. I know. This is why I can't take

men too seriously. They put you through all kinds of shit, and if you let them, they'll drive you crazy. Is there anything I can get you?"

"A new heart?" Bronze said jokingly.

"Sweetie, if I could, you know I would."

"I know. Call me later, okay?"

"Okay. And hey, we'll get through this," Angela assured her.

Chapter 31

Bronze had the strongest urge to see Julian. They had shared so many fun times together, and she desperately needed to hear his voice. Before she lost her nerve, she dialed his number. She prayed that he wouldn't hang up on her, even though he had every right to.

"Hello?"

"Julian, it's Bronze."

"Hi."

"Hi," she said simply. "Am I calling at a bad time?"

"Not at all. What's up?"

"I really need to talk to you. Can I see you?"

"Of course you can, Bronze. Do you want me to come pick you up?"

"Would you?"

"Just say when."

"In about half an hour?" she said.

"I'll be there."

"Oh, I almost forgot, Julian. I moved. I'm on Holloman Way, 379 Holloman Way."

"Okay. See you soon."

Shortly, Julian picked Bronze up, and they drove out to the lake. Before she knew it, she was spilling out her heart and soul. Julian let her talk without interruption, and when he finally did speak, he was careful not to badmouth his cousin.

"Come here," he said, taking her into his arms. She cried even harder. He stroked her hair and rocked her gently.

"Bronze, sometimes, we men can be *real* dogs. Love isn't fair. We just have to accept it for what it is—good, bad, or indifferent—and go with it. And life isn't fair. Nobody ever said it was. But time heals all wounds, and one day this will be behind you, and you'll go on with your life. Look at that beautiful sky. Whenever I get bogged down in my own problems, I come out here and lie under the stars. It gives me a totally new perspective and makes me realize just how minuscule I am in the vastness of the universe. If you remember nothing else that I've said to you, remember this: life owes you nothing. Be thankful that you're alive. And realize that you have a purpose for being here. Don't wallow in self-pity. Find your dream and go for it. Be happy."

"I thought he was different. That's what hurts most. But he's just like all the rest." She dried her eyes. "Enough about me. What's going on with you?"

"Work is good," Julian said. "I'm Millard's number three cover artist."

"That's fantastic!"

"Problem is, my ex all of a sudden wants me to just pick up and move to Atlanta, so I can help raise our daughter. I'd have to start my career all over again from scratch. I don't know, Bronze. Maybe I'm being selfish. I have a lot on my mind." He exhaled.

"I know the feeling," she agreed.

* * *

Bronze had been preoccupied with thoughts of Julian all day long. As if reading her mind, he called her that evening, and they agreed to meet at his apartment after work.

"Are you hungry?" he asked.

"Famished."

"Let's order a pizza."

"With everything on it," she added.

"Yes, everything," he agreed.

One large pizza and three root beers later, Julian and Bronze collapsed on his couch.

"Boy, I'm stuffed," Bronze said.

"That makes two of us. Nothing like pizza to help you make it through the rough times. I almost forgot. I have a surprise for you," he said, rising to his feet.

"What is it?" she asked.

"You'll see." He returned with a large shopping bag. "For you," he said simply.

She removed a heavy cardboard box from the bag and opened it. Inside was a portrait, the exact likeness of Bronze.

"Oh my goodness, Julian. It's me! When did you do it? *How* did you do it?"

"I started it the night I hurt you so badly after the party. It took months to finish because I had to do it from memory. I wanted to get it just right. I hope you like it."

"*Like* it? Julian, I *love* it! It's beautiful. You are a true artist. Thank you so much." She inhaled as he wrapped his arm around her. She buried her face in his neck loving the smell of his cologne. Julian looked down at Bronze, and their eyes met. She kissed his lips. "Make love to me Julian."

"Bronze, this isn't a good idea. I better take you home." Julian stood.

"Why? As long as we use condoms."

"Why?" he repeated. "Bronze, you've been through a lot. What kind of friend would I be if I took advantage of your vulnerability? You don't really want me. You just think you do. You're confused and just reaching out to me because I make you feel safe, but you're still in love with Brandon. I'm not gonna lie to you, Bronze. The thought of you in Brandon's bed turns my stomach. When he first told me about you, I was so jealous I couldn't see straight. I figured you hadn't told him about us and that if I did, you two would be history. But I realized that I couldn't give you what you needed and that he could, so I kept my mouth shut."

"I wanna thank you for keeping our secret, Julian. I know it couldn't have been easy for you. But now I'm asking you to give *us* a chance."

"We both know what we'd be dealing with if we were to get involved, Bronze, and frankly, I'm not sure you could handle it."

"Thanks for the vote of confidence."

"Don't take it like that," he said gently. "But I hurt you once, and I promised myself that I'd never hurt you again."

"I'm a big girl now." She rose to her feet and began unbuttoning her clothing.

"Come on, Bronze. Don't do this."

"Can you honestly tell me that you don't want me?"

"I've wanted you from the first moment I laid eyes on you, Bronze. We both know that."

"Then make love to me, Julian."

Chapter 32

After shedding many tears over Brandon, Bronze decided that life does, indeed go on. It wasn't always easy, but there was really no other alternative. The night before her birthday the old gang from Hubert's Northeast took her out to dinner. Dawn, Liz, and Monique were thrilled to see her. They played catch-up, filling Bronze in on the latest. Bronze simply told them that she and Brandon were no longer engaged, that things had been moving too fast, and they both needed some space. No questions were asked. They enjoyed their meal and promised not to wait so long to see one another again.

Bronze felt as though she had put up a good front at dinner, but deep down inside she was miserable. Every night since the break up she had cried herself to sleep, and it was still an effort to get out of bed in the morning. Half the time she went without makeup and swept her hair back in a ponytail.

Bronze never worked on her birthday. She and Stephanie went out to breakfast and then to the mall. It was tradition.

"Happy birthday, sweetheart," Stephanie said.

"Thanks, Ma." Normally a breakfast person, Bronze barely touched her Belgian waffles.

"Would you rather order something else?"

"I just haven't had an appetite lately. Can we skip the mall and go home?"

"Of course we can. It's your day."

Stephanie drove the short distance home. Once inside, Bronze burst into tears.

"It's so hard, Ma. I'm trying to be strong, but it still hurts."

"I know, sweetheart. I know. Nobody said life was easy." They sat in the kitchen, and Stephanie made herbal tea.

"Last month I thought I'd be spending my birthday with Brandon, and now I'm all alone. I don't mean you don't count, Ma. I just thought Brandon would be a part of my life."

"I know what you mean, Bronze," she said gently.

"I think I'll go take a nap. I feel like sleeping in my old bed."

"It's ready and waiting."

Bronze walked into her old room and looked around. Everything was just as she had left it. She lay down on her bed and thought about the events of the past few weeks. Fresh tears stung her eyes, chasing each other down her cheeks. She wiped her chin with her wrist, grabbed a tissue from the nightstand, and blew her nose. Eventually, she drifted off to sleep.

When Bronze woke up it was dinnertime. From her bedroom window she could see that her mother was out in the backyard, grilling barbecued chicken and burgers. The smell was delicious. They ate under the umbrella, enjoying the sunshine and summer air.

Stephanie gave Bronze an ankle bracelet and matching toe ring. She loved them. Later, they had chocolate cake and ice cream.

"Well, Ma, I'm getting ready to go. I have to work tomorrow."

"All right, Bronze. Why don't you take some dinner and cake with you?"

"Okay." She fixed a plate and gathered her things. Stephanie rose to get her keys, but Bronze stopped her. "I'll take the bus, Ma. It will be here in just a few minutes." She was home in no time.

Brandon's car was parked in front of Bronze's building. When she got off the bus, she spotted him immediately.

"What are you doing here?" she asked.

"We need to talk."

"Brandon, I have nothing to say to you, and there's nothing you can say to me. So what's the point?"

"Just give me a few minutes, Bronze. That's all. Can I come in? Please?"

"Brandon don't make this hard for me." Her eyes searched his. Finally, she succumbed and let him in.

"Bronze, I'm sorry. I'm so sorry. I didn't mean to hurt you. I was a fool. Capricia means nothing to me. You're my everything."

"Well, you sure couldn't prove it by that tape!"

"Bronze, I had had too much to drink that night. One thing led to another, and before I knew it we were in bed. It was just sex."

"Just sex? Just sex? How the hell do you expect me to respond to that, Brandon? Just sex. What, I wasn't enough for you? You had to have her too?"

"Of course you were enough. You were more than enough for me. It just happened."

"Just happened? You men are a trip. You always want to act like things are out of your control. Like you've been victimized. Nothing just happens. You chose to make it happen. You had a choice. You made your bed, now lie in it."

He grabbed her by the waist and pulled her to him. "I need you in my bed."

"Get off me. You think you can just waltz in here, mumble a few words, and I'm just supposed to take you back? You hurt me, Brandon. I can't even trust you anymore."

"You're right, Bronze. You're absolutely right, but can you look me in the eye and tell me you don't still love me?"

"Like the song says, "What's love got to do with it?"

"Don't be hard, Bronze. That's not you."

"Oh, you think you know me? I sure as hell don't know you. How could I possibly consider marrying a man I can't even trust? Maybe we were both wrong about each other. Maybe things worked out for the best."

"Let's both be honest, okay?"

She refused to look at him.

"I need you, Bronze. You're under my skin. You're in my blood. You're in my heart. I can't get you out of my system. I know I'll never find another woman like you. I'm miserable without you. That's why if I could take back what I did, I would in a heartbeat."

"Why, because you were caught?"

"No, because what I did jeopardized our relationship, and I never want to risk losing you again. Bronze, I promise, if you take me back, I will spend the rest of my life making it up to you. You're my world, my princess."

Bronze searched his eyes for some hint of truth. She wanted so desperately to believe him, but she was afraid of getting hurt again. Before she realized it, the tears were beginning to fall and she was in his arms letting him kiss them away.

"I love you, Bronze." He planted kisses all over her face and neck. Then, he took her engagement ring out of his pants pocket and placed it back on her finger. She gazed up into his eyes and smiled not remembering when she had been so content.

Bronze and Angela had made reservations one evening after work at the Black Thai Restaurant. Since they both loved Thai food, it was a great way to catch up on the happenings in each other's lives over the delectably spicy cuisine.

"So what's been happening with you lately?" Bronze asked Angela.

"Nothing but overtime. That's all I've been doing. We're pushing for a January premiere of *Voila!*, and I've been working my butt off."

"Brandon and I are back together. So before you call me a fool. . . ."

"I'm not going to call you a fool, Bronze. You're my girl. I just want you to be happy. Don't worry about what other people think."

"Brandon all but got down on all fours and begged my forgiveness. He promised to never cheat on me again. I know this might sound naïve, but I believe him. I was miserable without him. So, I took him back as long as he didn't pressure me into setting a date. I needed time to breathe. Enough about me. What's been going on with you?"

"You know I've finally reached a point in my life where I'm tired of giving out free samples. I'm ready for something more, but most of these men don't even know what they want. It's always stick and move. Believe it or not I've been celibate for ninety-two days."

"That's gotta be a record. I'm proud of you, lady."

"But you know, I still keep one stashed away on the side. Just in case."

"For emergency purposes. I understand." Bronze laughed and Angela joined in. "So how are Mom and Dad? I haven't seen them in ages."

"They're fine. Mom just retired last month. And Daddy said it's getting harder and harder for him to get up every morning while Mom just rolls over, so he might not be too far behind. How's your mom doing? Is she still seeing the tennis instructor?"

"Yeah. They're still quite an item. There's nothing like a good man to put a smile on a woman's face. It's really nice to see her happy and enjoying life for a change."

"Yeah, I know what you mean. Here's to happiness," Angela said, raising her glass and clinking it with Bronze's.

"Yes. To happiness," Bronze agreed.

It wasn't long before the news of Bronze and Brandon's reconciliation made its way back to Capricia in Atlanta. It hit her with a vengeance, and she vowed to break up the happy couple if it was the last thing she did.

She seized the opportunity when she became privy

to a juicy bit of information, and she couldn't wait to share it with Brandon.

"Hello, Brandon."

"What do you want, Capricia?"

"How's that little princess of yours doing?"

"Don't worry about it."

"Just thought you should know that your fiancée is screwing around on you. And you'll never guess with whom."

"Look, I don't have time for your games."

"My sister's girlfriend lives in Julian's apartment building. And those walls are pretty thin. She overheard Julian and Bronze knocking boots. And from what I understand, he's rocking her world."

"You can't stand the fact that it's over between us and that I've moved on. You'll say anything just to break up Bronze and me, won't you?"

"If you're so sure I'm wrong, why don't you ask Julian? Or better yet, ask your princess."

"Unbelievable. Good-bye, Capricia," he said, shaking his head as he hung up the phone.

Chapter 33

Stephanie had no relief from those annoying phone calls, but then she was thrown for another loop. One morning she received a plain white envelope in the mail. No stamp and no return address. Just a business-size envelope with her name neatly printed on the front. She quickly tore it open, anxious to examine its contents. It contained recent photos of her and Bronze. For a moment she went totally numb. Whoever was behind all this knew where she lived. Maybe it was time she contacted the police.

Stephanie had just returned from a wonderful evening of dinner and dancing with Ross. As paranoid as she was about getting her hopes up when it came to men, a small voice within couldn't help but wonder if something serious was brewing. It had been quite some time since she felt this way about a man. Not only were they lovers, they were friends. She genuinely enjoyed his company, whether it was on the tennis court or lounging around the house with fresh bagels and coffee on a Sunday morning.

Since he was a full-time biology teacher, they shared a love and respect for academics. Sometimes they would debate for hours on end the nature versus nurture question. Stephanie felt that environment was the key to development, whereas Ross felt that everything boiled down to heredity. They'd argue back and forth until one called a truce, but the next time they'd eagerly pick up where they left off. Fueled and ready to go again.

Sometimes they'd go away for a couple of days, and Stephanie would have to remind Bronze that *she* was still the mother when Bronze would greet her with twenty questions upon her return.

In fact, Stephanie had just returned from a few days in the mountains with Ross when her ringing phone welcomed her home. It was him. He cut to the chase. That was his style.

"Be at the uptown library tomorrow morning," he said.

"You're crazy!"

"If you're not there, you and your daughter will be sorry. Trust me."

"Don't threaten me," she said before hanging up.

He called right back. "I'll expect you at ten o'clock sharp, and come alone."

"How will I recognize you?" she asked.

"You won't. I'll recognize you. That's all you need to know." With that he hung up.

There was no one to turn to. Stephanie panicked. That night she broke out in a cold sweat. She reached for her Bible for strength and consolation. She hardly slept a wink, awaking exhausted the next morning.

Without any breakfast she showered and prepared to leave the house, certain she would be unable to keep her mind on traffic, which, thank God, was light.

She didn't realize how tightly she had been gripping the steering wheel until she reached the library's parking lot. Her knuckles were virtually yellow. She checked her watch. It was only nine-thirty. What was she going to do until ten o'clock? She sat in her car watching the tiny secondhand and trying to imagine what "the voice" looked like. Could it be that thirty-something-looking man with the torn jeans and T-shirt or the middle-aged man in the suit getting out of his parked car? Stephanie had no idea. They both looked benign enough. She checked her watch again. It was nine fifty-five. Time to go inside.

Stephanie hadn't the slightest idea exactly where in the library they were to meet. She found an empty table toward the rear, thankful that it was not an exceptionally large building.

The big clock over the librarian's desk read seven minutes after the hour. She was perspiring, and her clothes began to cling to her body. But sweaty palms and all, Stephanie had no choice but to sit and wait.

Finally, around ten-fifteen a tall, thin man in a cheap, dark brown suit approached her table. So this was him. He was about as pale as they came, and she silently compared him to Ross's well-tanned body. He wore thick glasses, and Stephanie's first thought was of a turtle. Even with glasses, his eyelids were at half-mast. He sat down at the table.

"Okay, what's this all about?" she whispered.

"Let me get straight to the point, Ms. Sutton. It's

very simple. I have some information that could be . . . shall we say, scandalous in the wrong hands. Unless you and I can make a deal."

"Listen, you've been harassing me for months. And I'm supposed to believe you have something on me? What do you take me for—a fool? I should call the cops right now. I could have you arrested so fast it'll make your head spin."

"You don't seem to understand. I'm calling the shots. Not you. Got it?" He grabbed her wrist and squeezed it. She was surprised that a man so thin harbored such strength, but she wiggled free.

"Don't touch me. Do not ever touch me again. You got that?"

"Ms. Sutton, I think we're getting away from our purpose for meeting here today."

"And what if I don't cooperate?" Stephanie asked.

"That's up to you, but be prepared to suffer the consequences."

He reached into his breast pocket and laid three pictures of Bronze on the table. "Such a beautiful daughter." His voice trailed off. "I wouldn't want anything to happen to her." He smiled and his eyes looked like two slits.

Stephanie took a good, long look at the sorry excuse for a man. She wanted nothing more than to spit in his face and run—run from him, and more importantly, from her past. But she had to stay and protect her daughter. Just as she had tried to protect Bronze since the day she was born. The façade was crumbling right before her very eyes, and there appeared to be no way of saving it. She wanted to scream but dared not. She tried to stand, but her legs would not support her. Stephanie could hear her mother's voice: "Bronze has a right to know the truth." Stephanie never denied that, but somehow in twenty-six years she never found quite the right moment.

Everything began to blur. She didn't know how she made it home in one piece. She was dazed. She climbed into bed, realizing that sleep would be her only freedom.

Chapter 34

Capricia showered, dressed, and prepared for work. She was already running behind schedule, and she knew she'd hear it from her uncle when she got there.

Congressman Robert Carson ran a tight ship, and the closer it came to Election Day, the tighter the ship. Whoever said she got her job through nepotism was sadly mistaken. If anything, she was over-qualified as an administrative assistant, but until something better came along, she was stuck with Uncle Rob.

Lucky for her he was not yet there when she arrived. In fact, no one was. Capricia opened up the office, put on a pot of coffee, and began opening the mail. There was a stack of campaign contributions, which meant that she would have to take a trip to the bank to deposit them.

Capricia's mind drifted to thoughts of Brandon and Bronze. She was preoccupied with destroying them by any means necessary. One thing for sure, her next move would have to be brilliant, and she'd consider it from every possible angle before executing it. This time she wouldn't fail. Drastic results called for drastic measures.

Capricia got back to the task at hand, opening mail and then drafting a speech for the congressman. She was interrupted by a good-looking Federal Express carrier. Boy was he wearing that uniform. She signed for the envelope and watched him and his tight buns walk out the door.

Though the envelope from A.T. Winters was addressed to her uncle and marked *Confidential,* Capricia didn't let that stop her from opening it. She was so engrossed in the documents that she almost missed the photo of a mother and daughter. By the time she skimmed the second page, her mouth dropped open. "Well I'll be damned."

Angela heard the familiar thud of the newspaper hitting the front door before she could roll out of bed and place both feet on the floor. She retrieved the newspaper and put on a fresh pot of coffee. As usual she turned to Paige Lawson's column first. She browsed through it until something of interest caught her eye.

Lately, there had been a lot of talk about the race for Congress in Atlanta's sixteenth district. Since Angela had personally met Councilman Malone in D.C., she took a special interest in the race. Leave it to Paige Lawson to get straight to the point.

Angela couldn't imagine what kind of dirt was being flung at the councilman as self-assured and well-rounded as he appeared, but then again everyone had skeletons in the closet. It sure would be interesting to unveil his. Perhaps in a juicy magazine article. That certainly would earn Angela more respect around the office and another byline. After all, she wasn't trying to be a one hit wonder. She quickly showered and readied herself for work.

Winters had also read Paige Lawson's column about mudslinging. It did not surprise him in the least, since he was the one who contacted her in the first place. He hadn't leaked the entire story, just enough to peak Lawson's curiosity. And it had worked. Already, Malone's ratings had fallen a few percentage points. And when Winters finished with Malone, he'd probably drop out of the race altogether. All Winters had to do was sit back and play his hand. And that's exactly what he intended to do.

Councilman Malone was being interviewed by Atlanta's local television station WDJP. The reporter, Jessica Deer, was interviewing him on the plight of the homeless as well as his plans to reduce their ranks. He shared his concerns on this disenfranchised segment of the population. He stressed the importance of housing and employment second, only to a program designed to restore their self-esteem. After all, most people were not born homeless and needed a means to reconnect with mainstream society. Lastly, he addressed the issue of homeless children who were tragically falling through the cracks. All in all, Malone presented quite a polished front, and Jessica Deer wished him well in the election.

With that behind him, Malone concentrated on his next appointment, which was a speech he was giving at a dinner sponsored by the Atlanta chapter of the African-American Professional Network. There were so many things one had to do as a politician, but that was the life he had chosen. He gave his speech, shook hands, took pictures, and prepared to leave.

Fourteen-hour days took their toll no matter how ambitious he was. Once home he crashed. Somewhere in the twilight between that moment of sleep and consciousness it came to him clear as crystal: eight six seventy six. He quickly sat up in bed. Of course. Why hadn't he thought of it sooner?

Chapter 35

Bronze and Brandon's evening at Ebony's was a much-needed night out. They had both been putting in a lot of overtime at work and welcomed the chance to do some clubbing. That night they shared good food, good music, and good conversation. Bronze was quite content with her man by her side. When they were together, no one else mattered. Their eyes locked as Brandon said in a husky voice, "Let's get outta here." Bronze was right behind him. In the interest of time they went to his apartment as it was closer than Bronze's place. Once inside they got right down to business.

He kissed her hard, his tongue searching hers out. They slid over to the couch, and she sat on top of him, one knee on each side of his hips. Brandon snapped open her top with one swift motion revealing her twins, which he could not wait to devour. With another swift motion he unhooked her bra, freeing them.

Bronze continued kissing him, her fingers playing with his right nipple until she replaced them with her mouth. He let out a moan, running his hands through her hair. She stood and wiggled out of her miniskirt, throwing it on the floor along with her moist panties. Bronze was now stark naked. She looked down at him on the couch, willing him with her eyes to stand so she could undress him too. She smiled, loving the effect she had on his manhood.

Brandon wasn't about to object as he watched his clothes and underwear join hers in a heap on the floor. Bronze jumped into Brandon's arms, flinging her legs around his middle as he carried her into his bedroom. He couldn't get her into his bed fast enough. She was all over him, touching him, caressing him, tasting him. He could always tell when she was ready for him. Her kisses became harder and deeper as though she wanted to ram her tongue down his throat. And if that wasn't enough, her vagina tried to squeeze the life out of his finger. Damn, she was so wet. She was definitely ready.

Brandon was in a teasing mood. He pulled his mouth away from hers and reintroduced himself to the twins, playing with one and then the other. He couldn't decide which one he liked better. From there he went south to her thighs skipping over where he knew she wanted him the most. He rolled her over on her stomach and relished the tiny dimples behind her knees. She grabbed him by the head and pulled him north. He got the message.

Finally, he rolled her over on her back, wanting to give it to her the way she loved it best. Some women preferred being on top, but not Bronze. She loved lying underneath him. He slid right into her and made himself at home. Wet and tight. Just the way he liked it. She wrapped her legs around him, and he went in even deeper. He felt good being all up in there. He wanted to cum, but she wasn't ready and he wanted to please her the way she pleased him.

"Oh yes," she said, panting. "Right there. Don't stop. Please, don't stop."

"Whose is it? Is it mine?" he asked her.

"It's yours, baby."

"Is it *all* mine?"

"It's yours, baby. It's *all* yours. Oh, Brandon, I'm cumming." Her sweaty body grew limp as he came too. He kissed her lightly on the lips while his dick crept out of her in slow motion.

She got up to get them something to drink, but he grabbed her from behind. "Hey, we're just getting started."

Chapter 36

Stephanie had just said good night to Ross and finished up the dinner dishes when her phone rang. It was Bronze.

"What's going on, Ma?"

"You just caught me, honey. I'm getting ready for a nice, long bubble bath. I could soak for hours."

"Did Ross come by for dinner?"

"Yeah. He just left."

"You guys have been seeing a lot of each other lately."

"We enjoy each other. I feel bubbly and alive when we're together. He's very special."

"Is he seeing anyone else?"

"I don't think so, but then again with men you never really know for sure."

"Well, I think the two of you are good together. You deserve to be happy, Ma."

"Thanks, hon. Let me go before the tub overflows."

"Okay, Ma. Talk to you later."

Stephanie rushed into her bathroom and turned off the faucet. Scented bubbles filled the tub, and she quickly readied herself for a nice, long soak. The water was as hot as she could stand it. With a neck cushion and a glass of white zinfandel by her side, she unwound. The water relaxed her body as well as her mind. She sat back and imagined Ross in the tub with her. His magic touch always made her feel wonderful. Sometimes he'd massage her neck and feet. God, she loved that man's touch. How she needed it right now with all the turmoil and tension in her life. She sipped her wine. What was she going to do?

The telephone rang and though she was within arms' reach of the cordless phone, she almost decided against answering it.

"Hello?"

"Hello, Stephanie."

She recognized his voice instantly and was taken aback. There were some things that even time could not erase. If only.

"Are you still there?" he asked, breaking the silence.

"Yes," she said simply, not knowing what else to say.

"I need to see you," he said urgently.

"Yes, I know." She hesitated. They agreed upon a time and place and hung up.

Stephanie's heart was racing. Suddenly, she needed to talk with her mother more than she needed a bubble bath. As the bubbles headed down the drain, she wondered if her relationship with Bronze would too.

He contemplated his future as he lay across the bed. Without blinking, he stared straight up as if miraculously the solution to all his problems would appear on the ceiling before his very eyes.

He relived the anguish that brought him to this point

in his life. He would never forget the look in his bride's eyes when she caught him in bed with his male lover.

He knew there was no way to erase that tape. It was forever etched in his memory with indelible ink, and no amount of alcohol could anesthetize his pain.

Guilt. For too many years he had turned his anger inward, allowing it to seep into his being until it colored every cell with its ashiness. At times it numbed him, crippling his emotions. At other times he was driven by it as though somehow through his ambition, he could find the atonement his soul so desperately sought. He was a modern-day Judas, betraying his flesh and blood for his own selfish gain.

He cursed his bisexuality and the day he was born. If only he were totally gay. But through no fault of his own, he straddled the fence. Sometimes preferring women. Other times preferring men. Never able to fully commit to either one. He knew his life would be so much less complicated if he could choose one over the other. But no, he had to choose both and destroy lives in the process. More lives than he cared to admit.

Not a single day escaped him without thoughts of his daughter, born August 6th, 1976. Today was no exception. Years ago he had abandoned her for the sake of his own survival. Now, would he be forced to abandon his future for the sake of hers? More importantly, would he be truly willing and able to make that sacrifice? He knew that one day he would come face-to-face with his past. Yes, he'd look it straight in the eye. And then what?

On any other day Bronze would have called her mother first before stopping by, but not today. She let herself in through the back door, but there was no sign of Stephanie in the kitchen or den.

"Ma?"

"In here, Bronze," Stephanie said from the living room. Bronze caught a slight hint of hesitation in her voice.

"I thought we could . . ." Bronze was at a loss for words. There in the living room big as day was Councilman Malone. Pleasantly surprised, Bronze looked from him to her mother. Within seconds, however, her expression changed from sheer delight to utter disbelief.

"You two know each other? Wait a minute. What's going on?"

"Sit down, Bronze," Stephanie said.

Chapter 37

If there was one thing Stephanie Sutton disliked more than a blind date, it was a late blind date. She and her best friend Charlene Matthew were at a popular High Street bar after an Ohio State football game. Now granted, it was the last regular season game and OSU had beat the pants off their old rival, the University of Michigan, and the streets were jammed with traffic, but was that any excuse for Charli's boyfriend and a classmate of his to be thirty minutes late?

"So help me, Charli, if he's not here in ten minutes, I'm outta here," Stephanie warned.

"To do what? Go back to the dorm and read all those old love letters from Jack? Take it from me, Steph. He was a bum when he wrote them, and he's still a bum. But lucky for you he's somebody else's bum now. All I can say is good riddance!"

"What's this guy like anyway?"

"His name is Adam Malone, and he's in Bill's English lit class. Political science major, great sense of humor. Look, here they come now."

Bill did the introductions and the guys sat down.

"So what d'ya think of the game, Stephanie?" Adam asked.

"Seen one you seen 'em all," she said, somewhat flippant, not wanting to look directly at Adam.

Even by the time their burgers and fries arrived Stephanie's guard was still up. Charli and Bill headed for the dance floor, leaving Stephanie and Adam alone.

"You're even prettier than Bill and Charli said you were."

"Thank you," Stephanie said politely, not about to return the compliment.

Adam was what Stephanie called "playboy brown" with his smooth complexion and faint mustache. He had nice, broad shoulders which meant that he probably had a strong back. And through his jeans she sensed firm legs and a tight behind. She was certain that he was a favorite with the women, especially since a few were rubbernecking at that very moment. And if she hadn't been sitting right next to him, she'd more than likely be doing the same.

"Have you known Bill and Charli long?" Adam asked.

"Since freshman year. And you?"

"Just since fall quarter."

Charli and Bill returned to the table. "Hey, I got an idea," Bill said. "Let's all go roller-skating."

"You guys go ahead. I have some studying to do," Stephanie said.

"Oh, come on, Stephanie. It'll be fun," Charli said. "And we won't be out all night."

"Next time," Stephanie promised, getting up from the table, her burger only half eaten. She was anxious to return to the dorm. After all, maybe Jack had stopped by and left a note under her door.

"Well, it was nice meeting you, Stephanie," Adam said.

"Thanks," Stephanie said, nodding.

"I'll call you tomorrow," Charli said.

Stephanie returned to an empty dorm room. Her roommate was out partying, and there was no note from Jack. She sat on her bed thinking about him. She knew it would be a long time before she got him completely out of her system. The funny thing was that she wasn't one hundred percent certain that was what she wanted to do.

Weeks passed and Stephanie didn't hear one word from Jack. Obviously their relationship meant less to him. In her pain, food became a trusted ally. It never disappointed her. For breakfast she'd go to IHOP and order extra servings of buttermilk pancakes swimming in syrup. Lunch was usually a quick butterscotch milkshake between classes, while dinner normally consisted of another heavy, starchy meal. She became a pro at using food to self-medicate.

It didn't take long for the pounds to add up. In three months she gained twenty pounds. There were so many days when she was tempted to pick up the phone and dial his number. On one occasion she did just that. But when a woman answered the phone, she immediately hung up. The last straw came when Stephanie unexpectedly ran into Jack at the student union. The woman was a showstopper, and Stephanie felt like a hunk of cheese standing next to her. It pained her to see the look of disgust on Jack's face.

Later, when she returned to the dorm, the first thing she did was remove all the junk food from her room.

Out went all the candy bars and cupcakes and cookies. Deep down she knew it was time to break all of her emotional ties to Jack. Time to move on.

That night Stephanie went to bed feeling hopeful for the first time in months. She drifted off to sleep with visions of being in church. Elder Hopkins was preaching to the congregation. His message was simple: The Lord can give you much more than this! It seemed so real. Stephanie awakened with a jolt. When she went to church the following morning, Elder Hopkins preached on that very same subject. She sat stiffly in the pew as a feeling of déjà vu washed over her. *Well,* Stephanie said to herself, *here's your confirmation. It's time to let go and move on.*

With this new outlook, she slowly shed the unwanted pounds as she loaded up on fresh fruits and veggies. She took long walks on campus and concentrated on loving herself for a change. It seemed that she was always attracted to the wrong men, the pretty boys who always kept a little something, or rather someone, on the side. When would she learn that a good-looking man wasn't always the prize? One thing for sure, she was tired of being hurt. What had Jackie Kennedy said? She didn't trust handsome men? Neither did Stephanie.

She thought about Adam Malone. He was charming and sure of himself, but not arrogant. She liked that combination. He seemed like a fun person, but not someone who thought of himself as the cat's meow.

Little by little Stephanie flushed Jack out of her mind, but on occasion when she'd run into him, she was quickly reminded that he still held a fragment of her heart. However, she did notice that each time she ran into him the tugging on her heart lessened. With each tear she shed he became a part of her past, until finally, one day, he was gone.

As was typical of men, the moment Jack realized that her every thought was no longer of him, she became a challenge. Once again he became a frequent caller, eager to reconcile. No, she assured him, she wasn't playing games, she had simply grown immune to his sweet talking, and she would not give him another chance to break her heart. It bruised Jack's ego to say the least, but finally he, too, accepted the fact that it was over.

Stephanie returned to the dating scene. No one swept her off her feet, but men did provide an occasional diversion from her studies. She weighed her options. Was twenty percent of something better than one hundred percent of nothing? The problem was that there was no man she loved. And in Stephanie's mind that was indeed a monumental problem. From the moment she had her first kiss, there was always a love interest in her life, until now.

Sometimes she moped around her dorm for days, leaving only to attend classes. The big Valentine's Day dance was quickly approaching, and Stephanie did not and could not picture herself there. She could go with Charli and Bill. They had no problem with that, but that's not what she wanted. She was tired of being a tag along . Maybe she'd just stay home that night and curl up with a good book.

She ended up missing the big dance, opting to stay home instead. To her surprise, however, she had an unexpected visitor that night in the person, of none other than Adam Malone.

"Feel like company?" he asked as she opened her dorm door.

"Sure, why not? Come on in, Adam."

"Looks like I'm not the only one missing the dance tonight. What's your excuse?"

"I'm behind in my studying actually," she lied. "And yours?"

"My girlfriend's out of town for a while, so I figured I better lay low. Her girlfriends probably have the entire campus bugged, waiting for me to mess up so they can report to her when she returns."

"So how did I get so lucky to be graced with your presence?"

"Well, you're worth the risk." Adam smiled and winked at her. She returned his smile.

Ever since she had first met him after the football game, he had piqued her curiosity, but at the time she only had eyes for Jack. Now, Jack was completely out of her system, and she was ready to move on.

"So where's your boyfriend?" Adam asked.

"There's no such animal."

"You're joking, right? I mean the way you flew out of the club after the football game, I knew you were running into somebody's arms."

"We broke up."

"So you're available," he said it as a statement, not a question.

"Yes, and you're not," she teased.

"I may have a girlfriend, but I'm not dead."

"Famous last words."

"Touché." He laughed. "I'd love to take you out on a real date."

"What about your girlfriend?"

"Oh, she'll be gone for another week."

"I don't know, Adam. It's kind of sneaky."

"It'll be our little secret. Let's be honest, okay? You

and I are very much attracted to each other. So why don't we go out one evening and see what happens. We might hit it off, or we may have a lousy time. Let's give it a chance. Deal?"

"Deal," she said.

Saturday night arrived and Stephanie prepared herself for a date with Adam. She rummaged through her closet a dozen times in search of *the* outfit. She must have tried on three different ones until she decided on the peach sweater and skirt set she knew perfectly complemented her golden-brown complexion.

Stephanie was ready a full hour before Adam was due to pick her up. She used the extra time to touch up her manicure and redo her hair. She couldn't decide which style looked most appropriate. She combed her hair into a French twist a la Holly Golightly from *Breakfast at Tiffany's,* but it reeked of high expectations for the evening. Finally, she settled on a flip. It was simple without looking overdone or pretentious. She took care of the finishing touches as she heard the phone ring in the hall.

There was a light tap at the door. It was Beth from down the hall. The phone call was for Stephanie.

"Hello?"

"Hi, Stephanie. It's Adam. I don't quite know how to say this, but I'm sorry I can't see you tonight. It wouldn't be right. I wouldn't be able to respect myself cheating on Faith. I mean, if the shoe were on the other foot, would you appreciate being treated like this?"

"No, I wouldn't, Adam. You're probably right, and I have to respect you even more for your decision. But you know, I am disappointed."

"Same here, Stephanie. I was really looking forward to our date. But I hope you understand."

"Of course I do, Adam. Don't worry about it." She hung up feeling empty and alone. Stephanie quickly dialed Charli's number, explaining to her what had just happened.

"I know how you feel, Steph, but at least you know he's a man with honesty and integrity. And there are so few of them around. Keep your chin up. It's not the end of the world. And between you and me, I don't think everything's rosy between Adam and Faith anyway."

"What makes you say that?"

"Let's just say a little birdie told me. And that's all I'm gonna say on that tonight."

A month passed and Stephanie heard nothing from Adam. She assumed that he was still involved with Faith, even though Charli had told her they were on shaky ground.

And then the unexpected happened three weeks before graduation. She ran into Adam at an OSU basketball game. He was wearing a pair of old worn-out jeans and a cotton shirt, and when their eyes locked from across the arena, he had the most charming look on his face. By the time the final buzzer went off, the distance between them was cut in half. They finally met on the arena floor amid other Buckeye fans dizzy from the game's excitement. The Buckeyes had led by seventeen points at the half only to win by one point.

"So," Adam began, "it's great to see you, Stephanie." He couldn't stop grinning.

She looked him over from head to toe in one easy

glance, definitely pleased with the view. "Thank you," she said, smiling up at him.

"Are you here alone?"

"Uh-huh."

"Great! Why don't we go grab a bite to eat? My treat."

"I'd love to."

Stephanie and Adam ended up in a quaint little coffee shop on High Street. She was too excited to eat, ordering a cup of coffee instead. Adam, on the other hand, was famished, ordering a cheeseburger deluxe. She sat across from him wondering if he and Faith were still an item.

As if reading her mind, Adam brought up the subject. "I guess you know that Faith and I broke up," he said, wiping his mouth.

"No, I didn't," she said with what she hoped was just the right amount of concern.

"Yeah. It was a mutual decision. We both finally realized that we're better as friends than lovers. So that's that."

Stephanie looked at Adam, noticing the tiny scar above his left eyebrow. He certainly was a looker, she thought, not realizing that he was thinking the same thing. When Adam finally broke the silence, Stephanie knew without a doubt that Adam Malone would be the next man with whom she'd become involved.

"Now that your boyfriend and Faith are both history, maybe we can make some headlines of our own," he said.

"Time will tell," she answered.

"I'm sure it will," he agreed.

* * *

After graduation Stephanie opted to stay in Columbus. She had been accepted as a temp at the Twinkle Toes Nursery, a job that she easily learned to love. Her daily interactions with four-year-olds soon revealed her maternal instincts, a revelation that surprised Stephanie more than anyone else.

She and Adam had been dating for a couple of weeks when he informed her of his plans to go to law school in the fall. That summer he took a job working with Councilman Wade McKay to supplement his income. He wrote press releases and called constituents by day, and tried to make time with Stephanie by night.

The more time they spent together, the more they enjoyed each other's company. At Adam's suggestion, they began double dating. Stephanie was not thrilled with this suggestion, but she never let him know it. After a while she was convinced he'd see that by double dating, he was only prolonging the inevitable, not preventing it.

On one particular night Adam and Stephanie were joined by his friend Jerry and Jerry's girlfriend, Roberta, at the Music Box. A new group that called themselves Heart was performing there for the first time.

After the concert while Adam assumed the double date would continue, Jerry and his girlfriend brought it to an end, which left Adam and Stephanie alone. Secretly, Stephanie was thrilled. And in his own way, so was Adam.

Adam offered to take Stephanie home, and she agreed. He kissed her good night at the door, all the while wishing that she would invite him inside. He acknowledged her sensuality and desire through her clothing. When Stephanie finally closed the door behind her and he was left standing outside, Adam laughed to himself, convinced that his days alone were numbered.

When the fall quarter rolled around in September, Adam resumed his studies. He spent so many evenings in the law library that he hardly had time for Stephanie. One day after canceling lunch for the umpteenth time, Stephanie jokingly told him that he spent so much time with his law school buddies, that she was beginning to wonder about him.

"Jealousy," he said, laughing. "I'm flattered."

Stephanie found other ways to occupy her time. She was pleased to join the permanent staff of the Twinkle Toes Nursery in early October. The preschoolers as well as the rest of the staff loved her. She was patient with the kids, and they responded to her good nature.

One afternoon while the children were busy coloring, Stephanie had a visitor—Adam. She excused herself from the children for a moment, and her assistant took over. The two talked in the hallway as the children eagerly ran to the door, anxious to get a peek at Miss Sutton and her boyfriend. Their giggles and whispering amused Adam.

He told Stephanie that he'd be out of town for a few days. His father was quite ill, and he felt it was best to be there for his family. But he'd be back by the end of the week and promised to make time for her. Adam kissed Stephanie gently and waved good-bye to her class. When they realized that they had been spotted, the children dashed from the doorway and raced back to their seats. Stephanie smiled to herself and returned to the classroom. One thing for sure, when Adam returned, Stephanie would make certain that he'd realize all that he'd been missing.

The weekend rolled around before Stephanie knew it, and she was delighted to hear that Adam was back in town. He returned with good news. His father was recovering nicely from a heart attack and the prognosis was excellent. Stephanie had never been to the upscale Gold Dust Restaurant, so Adam made reservations to the four-star restaurant that Saturday night.

Stephanie already had on her coat when she greeted him at the door. As he entered the apartment, she closed the door behind him.

"We're running late, Steph. The reservations are for eight-thirty."

"I know, but I couldn't decide what to wear. What do you think?" she asked unbuttoning her coat and letting it fall to the floor. She wore a French cut, black lace teddy, and a black garter belt with stockings. "Is this okay? I hope I'm not overdressed." Slowly she began to remove her stockings.

Adam didn't say a word. He broke out in a sweat. To hell with the restaurant! Something told him they'd never make it there that night.

Stephanie went home for Thanksgiving and brought Adam along with her. She felt it was time for her family to meet him.

"Ma, this is Adam Malone."

"Adam, this is my mother, Mrs. Sutton."

"Pleased to meet you, ma'am," he said, shaking her hand.

"Stephanie, why don't you let Adam have your room, and you can sleep with me?"

"Sure, Ma. Where's Xavier and Vy?"

As if on cue Vy came out of the kitchen. "Stephanie!" She hugged her big sister. "Is this Adam?"

"Yes, Vy, this is Adam. And Adam, this is Vy. Where's Xavier?"

"Oh, he ran to the store to pick up a few last-minute things for me. As soon as he gets back, we can all sit down and eat. Stephanie, you're so thin!" her mother exclaimed.

"Doesn't she look great, Ma?" Vy asked.

"Great? She's practically skin and bones. All she needs are a few home cooked meals, and she'll look like a new person. I guarantee it."

Just then Xavier came through the door carrying a grocery bag. "Hey, sis. Good to see ya. You must be Adam," he said, extending his hand. "Nice to meet you, man."

"Same here," Adam answered.

"Mama, when are we gonna get some of that bird? I'm starving," Xavier said.

"Well, let's eat before you and Stephanie both collapse." They all headed for the dining room, their noses leading the way. Rose said grace. "I hope you're hungry, Adam," she said. "There's plenty, but leave room for dessert."

"This dressing is delicious, Mrs. Sutton," Adam said.

"I made it," Vy admitted proudly.

"It's amazing that someone who can't even boil water can make homemade dressing, isn't it?" Xavier teased.

"I'm glad you like it, Adam," Vy said, ignoring her brother.

They finished their Thanksgiving dinner. Adam was especially glad that he had left room for dessert. And what a dessert—homemade zucchini cake with cream cheese frosting.

The doorbell rang, and Stephanie got up to answer it. It was Joe and Minnie Grey from next door. They had been the Suttons' neighbors for more than twenty years. But they were more than neighbors; they were friends. The Greys were childless, and they always took a special interest in the Sutton children.

"Oh, it's so good to have you all together again," Mrs. Grey said.

"How long ya staying, Stephanie?" Mr. Grey asked.

"We're leaving Sunday morning. Speaking of we, this is my friend Adam Malone. Adam, this is Mr. and Mrs. Grey from next door."

"Nice to meet you both," Adam said.

"Likewise. I hope you're treating our girl well," Mr. Grey warned. "Because if not, you're gonna have to answer to me."

"To us you mean," Mrs. Grey added.

"She deserves the best," Adam said honestly.

"Then we're in agreement." Mr. Grey smiled.

"Why don't you two have some dessert. I have zucchini cake, and Joe, I made your favorite pound cake," Rose said.

Mr. Grey helped himself to a generous slice of pound cake. "I'll have to swim two hundred laps just to work this off, but believe me it'll be worth every stroke."

"I'll be right next to you, honey," Minnie said to her husband as she shoveled another piece of cake into her mouth. Never being ones to eat and run, the Greys stayed with the Suttons until late in the evening, reminiscing about old times.

After they left, the Suttons called it a night. Adam

went to sleep as soon as his head hit the pillow. Stephanie and her mother, on the other hand, sat in bed for a while talking.

"So, what d'ya think of Adam, Ma?" Stephanie eagerly asked.

Rose chose her words carefully. "He seems like a nice young man. How does he treat you?" she asked, throwing the ball back in Stephanie's court.

"I have no complaints except that he spends so much time in that law library. We're only ten minutes away from each other, but sometimes two weeks go by before I see him."

"And do you know what that's called, Stephanie?"

"What?"

"Ambition."

"But there's nothing wrong with ambition is there, Ma?"

"No, sweetie, nothing at all. As long as he controls it and doesn't allow it to control him."

"No, I can't imagine anything like that happening."

"Let's hope not."

"Good night, Ma."

"Good night, sweetie. It's good having you home."

"It's good being home, Ma."

With Thanksgiving behind her, Stephanie began preparations for Christmas. Her preschoolers drew Christmas trees and snowflakes to decorate classroom windows and doors, as well as made gifts for their parents out of coffee cans, yarn, and glue. The children were still at that magical age when they believed in Santa and his reindeer, so she and her assistant spent afternoons reading Christmas stories.

One Saturday afternoon Stephanie and Charli got together to do some holiday shopping. There were only two names left on Stephanie's list. She still had to buy for her mother and Adam. Shopping for her mother was not a problem. She'd already decided to buy her a pair of gold earrings, but shopping for Adam was another story. It was a toss up between an ID bracelet and a leather wallet.

"I'd go with the ID bracelet. And have it engraved. It's more personal," Charli advised her over hot cocoa. "A wallet's something you'd buy a neighbor or your grandfather. Not your boyfriend."

"I guess you're right."

"Of course I am. Are you and Adam going to his parents' for Christmas?"

"No. We're staying here. What about you and Bill?"

"We're spending Christmas in Ft. Lauderdale."

"You're kidding? When are you leaving?"

"The twenty-third."

"I can't imagine Christmas without snow. Must be all that Midwestern blood running through my veins," Stephanie told her Californian friend.

"While you're trudging through all that snow, just imagine me sunning myself on the beach. But back to the task at hand. D'ya know I still have presents to get? I hate these crowds. They make my flesh crawl. Let's finish up our shopping so we can get outta here."

Early Christmas morning Stephanie got up to call her family. All the circuits were busy, and she had to try several times before getting through. When she reached her mother, she and Adam had just finished their brunch. Yes, she missed them. No, she wasn't alone. Yes, she'd be home the next chance she got, and she loved her presents. The phone call was short and sweet. Stephanie promised to write.

Once Stephanie hung up with Rose she gave Adam her undivided attention. She noticed that he carried no package with him, and she concealed her disappointment quite well. Nevertheless, she gave him his gift as planned.

"I love it," Adam said simply. "Help me put it on. I guess you're wondering where your present is," he said.

"No, not really," she lied unconvincingly.

"Well, you should be. It's out in the hall. Let me bring it in for you," he said, opening the door of her apartment and returning with a large, square brightly colored box. He placed it at her feet.

Stephanie couldn't imagine what it might be. She hadn't a clue. Just as she attempted to pick it up and give it a shake, he told her that that wasn't a good idea, throwing her off the track even further.

Finally, she could wait no longer. She untied the big red bow and removed the lid. Inside the box was the most adorable honey-colored puppy. She lifted it out.

"Oh, how precious!" she squealed. "I love it. A puppy." She hugged it, loving the roundness of her newfound friend.

"Hey, where's my hug?"

Stephanie gave Adam a big hug and kiss though she was careful not to let go of the puppy. She cradled it in her arms like a baby. "It's adorable. What are we gonna name it? Is it a boy or a girl?"

"Can't you tell? It's a girl!"

"Well, she's precious. I love her already. How old is she?"

"About a month."

"She looks like her name oughta be Precious, so Precious it is." She put the puppy down on the floor. "Have I told you how much I love you?" she asked.

"No."

"Well, I do."

"All because of a puppy? If I'd known that I would've bought you a litter a long time ago."

"No, that's only part of it. But I guess it just put the icing on the cake. I've always wanted a puppy. I love you, Adam Malone."

"I love you, too, Stephanie Sutton."

That winter turned out to be a wonderful season for Stephanie and Adam. Though Adam had a heavy schedule at school that quarter, he refused to allow it to interfere with his relationship with Stephanie. The more he saw her, the more he wanted to be in her company.

Sometimes they'd take long walks with the puppy if the weather wasn't too bitter. Adam would share his hopes and dreams with Stephanie. One day he'd be a prominent corporate attorney with fancy clothes and a bank account to boot. And he'd earn more in a month than his father grossed in an entire year.

"Tell me about your childhood," Stephanie said.

"Well, I grew up in a modest home. There was always plenty of food and love. And that's all that really mattered. My mother's dream was to become a modern jazz dancer. She loved the arts and wanted to make certain that her only child was immersed in culture. I remember days when my parents would dodge the landlord and then rob Peter to pay Paul, just so they could afford to take me to the theater." Adam's thoughts drifted back to life in Dawnville.

Stephanie's voice brought him back to the present. "What did you say?" he asked.

"Sounds like you had a wonderful childhood."

"That I did," he admitted, grabbing her by the waist. "Last person inside has to make the cocoa."

Adam laughed, racing her back to her apartment. Life should be so easy.

Will and Amanda Malone were pleasantly surprised to hear from Adam one Wednesday evening. He called to let them know he had very important news to discuss with both of them, and that he'd be home that weekend. Not knowing what to expect, they were warned of the seriousness of the situation by the urgency in his voice.

Adam was not one to beat around the bush, and once home he got straight to the point. "I want to get married," he declared.

"Just like that? Out of the blue?" Mrs. Malone asked.

"You didn't get her in trouble, did you?" Will wanted to know.

"No, she's not pregnant."

"Then why the rush? I mean who is she, Adam? You haven't even brought her home," Mrs. Malone reminded him.

"She's a teacher, and we met at school. And I can't get her outta my mind."

"Is she the first girl you couldn't get out of your mind, Adam?"

"Of course not, Dad."

"Exactly. And she won't be the last. So finish law school. And if you decide that you still want to marry her, we'll give you our blessing. But right now the most important thing is your education. Let's be sensible," Will Malone said firmly.

"You don't understand," Adam told them. "I knew you wouldn't."

"Of course we do," Mrs. Malone said gently. "We were your age once."

"But you have to get your priorities straight. I don't want you to be a janitor like your old man. We want more for you, son. That's why we've been saving for your education since the day you were born. But I'm warning you right now, Adam. If you marry this girl. What's her name anyway?" Mr. Malone asked.

"Stephanie Sutton."

"If you marry Miss Stephanie Sutton, you can put yourself through the rest of law school. Count your mother and me out."

On March 24, 1975, Adam Malone and Stephanie Sutton were married by a justice of the peace in a small Columbus courthouse, with Charli and Bill as witnesses. It was a bitterly cold, wet day, but Adam and Stephanie refused to see it as a bad omen. They were young and in love and nothing could dampen their spirits or their future's outlook.

Adam explained to Stephanie right after his proposal the ultimatum his parents had given him in regards to cutting the purse strings. Stephanie had no desire to jeopardize her fiancé's future and wanted to postpone the marriage until after his graduation, but Adam wouldn't hear of it.

"I'll go to school during the day and just work evenings. You'll see. We'll manage. A lot of people do it. I'm young and healthy," he had told her.

But the truth of the matter was that Adam hated being away from his bride. And after a couple of months, he decided to take a quarter off from school. Not permanently, he told himself, but just so that he could take off some of the edge. Adam continued working for Councilman Wade McKay, and his camp welcomed Adam's change in hours from evenings to full time. It wasn't long before Adam tossed his hat into the political arena by running for district leader.

One evening Adam invited his campaign advisor Richard Hamilton over for dinner. Rich was a bachelor, and the thought of having another one of Stephanie's home cooked meals delighted him. Stephanie made her famous beef stroganoff, and she was flattered by Rich's hearty appetite.

"I can see why you've put on a few pounds, Adam," Rich said jokingly. "To marriage," he said, raising his wineglass.

"Yes, to marriage," Adam agreed, looking at Stephanie. "There's nothing in the world like it."

"So, Richard, are you seeing anyone?" Stephanie asked.

"No one seriously," he told her. "I'm just waiting for the right one to come along. And she hasn't yet."

"Don't mind my wife, Rich. She thinks everyone should be married."

"Happily married," Stephanie added.

They finished their meal and headed for the living room. Stephanie stayed behind and cleaned up the kitchen, preferring that over boring talk of politicians and local government. Adam and Rich stayed up half the night planning strategies. In fact, when Stephanie turned in for the evening it was after midnight, and she left them making an outline for a speech that Adam would deliver to the rotary club the following week.

She tried to sleep, but the laughter from the living room kept her wide awake. Finally, Adam came to bed bringing impatience and a slight buzz from drinking with him.

He stripped off his clothes instantly. Adam mounted her without saying a word. And it was all over before she knew it. Stephanie pushed him off her and tried to go back to sleep. What was it about politics that made Adam so aggressive? she pondered, not liking this dark, unfamiliar side of him.

The following morning he greeted her with breakfast in bed as well as apologies for his inexcusable behavior the night before. He bathed her with kisses and promised that it would never happen again. She forgave him. Two days later he came home with two roundtrip tickets to Aruba.

"But we can't afford it," Stephanie insisted.

"Sweetheart, we never had a real honeymoon. You deserve it. We deserve it."

A week later Adam and Stephanie found themselves taking a moonlit stroll along the beach in Aruba. For four days and three nights they agreed to concentrate on no one and nothing but each other. They would stay in bed until noon or until they ran out of ways to please each other, and then head for the white, sandy beach.

On their last evening there, as Adam sat across from his wife over dinner, he couldn't help but notice the inner and outer beauty she possessed. He felt a tremendous surge of pride having her as his wife. He called Stephanie his bronze bombshell with her golden tan and sun-kissed skin. In fact, he had a strong desire to just wallow in it. And the white linen dress she wore only accentuated her beauty.

Several men in the hotel dining room nearly broke their necks trying to get a good look at Stephanie. Adam silently laughed to himself. After all, he always said he didn't want a woman whom everyone wanted. Yet, at the same time he didn't want a woman whom no one wanted either.

Stephanie's inner beauty, however, was what hooked him. She was totally devoted to him, and he knew it. He cherished Stephanie and vowed never to hurt her.

They said good-bye to lazy days in the sun, Bahama Mamas, and glorious sunsets. The first day Stephanie returned to work after their vacation, she realized that she had left the bedroom radio on.

She rushed home that evening in an attempt to intercept the radio before Adam did. He could be such a stickler about budgeting. Money was tight, and it didn't make sense to waste dollars on the electric bill. Particularly, since they were now in the red from the trip to Aruba.

Thank goodness he wasn't home, and she wouldn't have to hear his mouth. In fact, she wouldn't have to hear his voice at all that evening. He called to let her know he'd be home late and not to hold dinner. Was the honeymoon over? The phone rang and she jumped, startled for a moment.

It was Charli. Yes, she'd love some company. It had been a while since the two had seen each other or gotten the chance to chat. Marriage had changed the parameters of their relationship. That was to be expected. And they were both honest enough with each other to admit that.

Charli came by, and they talked about everything under the sun except Stephanie and Adam's marriage. Rose had warned her daughter of the importance of keeping what went on behind closed doors with her husband private. So Stephanie never shared with her girlfriend, or anyone else for that matter, the other side of Adam.

Adam's dark side became more prevalent the closer he got to the election. In fact, one night after a big fundraising dinner at the Stanton Hotel, he accused his wife of flirting with Rich Hamilton.

"You're crazy, Adam," Stephanie said, the anger rising in her voice as he drove home that evening.

"You made a complete fool of yourself. Throwing yourself at Rich like that."

"All we did was dance to one song."

"Yeah, and you were all over him. It was disgusting."

The argument continued as they entered their apartment.

"What's gotten in to you, Adam? Where's the man I married? You've been under too much pressure lately. Maybe you should think about dropping out of the election."

"Don't be ridiculous. I've worked too hard to drop out at this late date. And don't change the subject."

"The subject is this horrible person you're becoming. Sometimes I feel like I don't know you at all."

"No, the subject is your throwing yourself at Rich. It was sickening. I was embarrassed for you. Everyone noticed. Do you want him, Stephanie? Maybe that's why you've been so frigid lately. You've got the hots for Rich Hamilton!"

"Frigid? Don't flatter yourself, Adam. All you know how to do lately is a wham bam thank you, ma'am, so why don't you do us both a favor and sleep on the couch."

"My pleasure," he said, heading for the living room.

It was official. All of the votes had been tabulated, and Adam Malone was the new district leader of District 8 in Franklin County, Ohio. He, Rich Hamilton and the entire Malone camp watched as the results aired on WDAN-TV and exchanged congratulatory hugs.

Twelve blocks away, Stephanie Malone also watched as the election results were announced, so when her husband called with the good news she was already elated.

"Honey, we're going out for a victory celebration, and I want you with me." Stephanie could hardly hear him with all the excitement and cheering in the background.

"I'll pick you up in half an hour. And oh yeah, wear something gorgeous. I want to show you off tonight."

Mr. and Mrs. Adam Malone lived it up that night. The champagne flowed as freely as the pride in Stephanie's eyes as she danced with her husband. The faint scent of power, which she detected on him when they first met began to swell. She soon discovered that power, intermingled with confidence, proved to be one helluva aphrodisiac.

That night as they drove home, she could hardly keep her hands off Adam. *He may have slept on the couch last night,* she thought, *but tonight he'll be in our bed where he belongs.* The drought was over. She moistened at the thought.

Behind closed doors Adam practically tore off the little black velvet dress that clung to her body only moments before. His mouth searched hers until neither could stand anymore.

They slid into the bed, their bodies in perfect sync. Perhaps it was all the longing and pent-up desire that caused them to explode so quickly. They lay back in bed drenched in sweat, completely satisfied.

For the next month the Malones re-created their honeymoon, reluctant to part company in the mornings and eager to return home each evening. One day, however, Stephanie woke up feeling under the weather. So much so that she was almost tempted to take the day off as Adam suggested. Had it not been for the fact that her preschoolers were singing in their first concert, she would have stayed in bed.

"It's probably just a touch of cold. Serves me right for not wearing my hat the other day," she said, shrugging if off. "I'll be all right."

By the time the afternoon rolled around she still wasn't feeling up to par, so she made an appointment to see her doctor right after work. Once there the nurse explained to Stephanie that there had been a cancellation, and that the doctor would see her shortly.

After Dr. Parish checked her pressure and weight, he asked her what was troubling her. She complained of a sore throat and fatigue that had been going on for a couple of days. He ordered the routine blood work and urine test, but did not seem very alarmed.

"Can you prescribe something for my throat? I feel like I'm swallowing bricks."

"Why don't we wait for the results of the tests, and we'll take it from there, okay? In the meantime try gargling with a solution of cider vinegar and honey. That should relieve the soreness."

When Stephanie came home that evening, she said nothing to Adam about her visit with Dr. Parish. After all, it didn't make sense to alarm Adam at this stage of the game. Especially since it was probably just the flu.

They had a quiet dinner, and Stephanie turned in early. Adam didn't mention her leaving the radio on all day. He sensed that Stephanie just needed some tenderness that night. He held her and gently caressed her back and shoulders until she drifted off to sleep.

Two days later, Stephanie got the results of her tests. She was four weeks pregnant. Stephanie hung up the phone in the lounge not quite able to believe her ears. She was pregnant. She was going to be a mother.

She went into the ladies' room and looked herself over in the mirror, the happiness apparent in her eyes. Did she look different? Would she acquire that pregnant glow? She wanted to tell someone but thought it best to contain her mirth. Naturally, Adam would have to be told first. She prayed that he would be as excited as she.

Stephanie left school early that day since it was a special occasion, and she was certain that her assistant wouldn't mind. She decided on a candlelight dinner with all of Adam's favorite foods: steak, green bean almondine, buttermilk biscuits, and candied yams. She knew she wouldn't have time to make the German chocolate cake he had become addicted to, but those triple fudge brownies from the local bakery were the next best thing, and she was sure they would do grandly.

Stephanie took the long way home using the extra time to relish thoughts of motherhood. Adam wasn't expected home until later that evening, and she'd have plenty of time to get ready for her husband. She was tempted to go out and buy a new negligee then decided against it. She had a white pegnoir that she hadn't even worn yet, and besides, after dinner she wouldn't be wearing it very long anyway.

She smiled to herself pulling up into the driveway. She entered the apartment, taking off her shoes and heading into the bathroom. For the umpteenth time that day she examined herself in the mirror. God, she was pregnant. Barefoot and pregnant at that!

From the bathroom she could hear the faint sound of the bedroom radio. She had left it on again. Smiling to herself, she turned the knob and opened the door.

"Oh my God!" she said, her heart sinking. Stephanie was going to be sick. Adam and his campaign advisor Rich Hamilton were in bed.

"It's not what you think." Adam jumped up quickly, his male organ still swollen. Stephanie began hyperventilating. She ran to the bathroom, overcome with nausea. Adam ran after her.

"Get away from me. Don't touch me," she yelled at him.

"But I can explain."

"You disgust me, Adam."

"I love you, Stephanie."

"Just get out! We're through." Her thoughts flashed back to the night she laid in bed while Adam and Rich talked politics in the living room. Then she zeroed in on their lovemaking that evening. He had been particularly rough with her. So rough that it was too painful to even pee afterward, and she had to wait until the next morning. Now it all came together. She felt like a fool. The writing had been on the wall all along.

The next few days proved to be the most painful and difficult for Stephanie. She felt as though her heart had been ripped out of her chest. Not only did she have to decide what would be best for herself, she also had to decide what would be in the baby's best interest.

She made plans to get together with Adam to discuss their future—or lack thereof. They met at a coffee house on Maple and Main. Adam had moved out and was staying in a studio apartment about five blocks away. She preferred it that way.

They both ordered coffee and then sat in silence. So much had happened. Adam spoke first.

"Where do we go from here?"

"We don't, Adam. I can't go back to you now. It's over." She thought about the child growing inside of her. A child who would probably never know its father. "But I felt that you had the right to know I'm pregnant."

He reached quickly for her hand. She held it for a brief moment and then let it go. She was letting go of their life together as well.

"I'm sure you'll be a beautiful mother to our child. And I'll try hard to be a good father. I mean that, Stephanie."

"What are you talking about? We're through, Adam."

"Stephanie, you mean the world to me. You are the love of my life. Give me another chance. I love you so much. I want to be a father to our child. Don't leave me."

She suddenly turned cold, lowering her voice. "I

don't want my child to know his father is a faggot. Just forget you ever knew me. Does anyone know about your dirty little secret?"

"No. It would ruin my political career."

"Yes, and we certainly want to keep that intact, don't we? I'll make a deal with you, Adam. I'll keep your little secret from your family and the press, if you give me a divorce and promise never to try and contact me or the baby."

"Wait a minute, Stephanie. You want me to sell out my own flesh and blood to save my political ass? Are you crazy?"

"Adam, take it or leave it. It's all up to you." Stephanie looked at Adam, the tiredness evident in her eyes. In total defeat, he answered.

"All right, Stephanie, you win. I'll give you a divorce and promise to never bother you or the baby. I'm sure I've made your day."

"You're a smart man, Adam. I knew you'd come to the right decision. This is the best for all of us. You'll see. You can come by tomorrow evening and pick up the rest of your things. I won't be home until late. My lawyer is drawing up the papers as we speak. All you have to do is sign them."

"Oh, so you knew I'd agree? You know me too well."

"Apparently not well enough."

Ten days later the divorce was final. The ink was barely dry on the papers before Stephanie moved back home to Havenwood. She needed the love and support of her family. Rose welcomed her daughter and her dog Precious home with open arms. No questions asked.

On August 6, 1976, at 10:01 p.m., Bronze Sutton made her debut into the world. After twelve hours of labor, Stephanie was both exhausted and awed by her six-pound bundle.

Bronze. The name evoked memories of her Aruban honeymoon with Adam, a blissful time when she thought their love would last forever, and he referred to her as his bronze bombshell. It was the only way she'd allow Adam into her daughter's life. Her one and only way of sharing Bronze with him.

Looking down at her daughter, she prayed that one day Bronze would understand the circumstances surrounding her birth and not hate her. Was she being unfair to her child by denying her father? Stephanie wrestled with putting Adam's name on the birth certificate. In the end she chose not to. She had to be strong for her daughter. That much she knew. She vowed to give her daughter twice as much love to make up for Adam's absence. Each day Bronze grew more like her mother. Thank heavens for that, Stephanie decided.

Chapter 38

A stunned, teary-eyed Bronze sat in her mother's living room, the disbelief evident on her face as she stared from Stephanie to Adam and back again.

"I-I can't believe this," she said, holding back the tears. "Why didn't you tell me the truth, Ma? You could have said something."

"I know. Please don't hate me, Bronze. I always wanted to tell you. I just never knew how." Stephanie sobbed openly. "It's like I blinked and twenty-six years went by. When you were little I couldn't find the right words to explain it to you."

"And when I got older?"

"I was already living the lie. It was too late then, Bronze."

"Bronze, don't blame your mother. If you wanna blame someone, blame me. It was my fault. I'm the one who messed up," Adam admitted. "I . . . ."

"I need time to think," Bronze said, ignoring Adam and rising. She was suddenly very warm. "I gotta get outta here." She ran to the front door, fighting back tears. "I need time to think," she repeated. "Time to get myself together." She closed the door behind her, leaving Stephanie and Adam alone.

"Dear God, please, please don't let me lose my child. Don't let me lose my Bronze." She rocked from side to side as the tears dripped from her chin. Then she stiffened. "I should have told her sooner," Stephanie said quietly, collapsing in Adam's arms.

Bronze entered her empty apartment, closing the door behind her in an attempt to shut out the harshness of reality. She turned on no lights, preferring the darkness to engulf her thoughts. Bronze Sutton. Bronze Malone. Who was she? Could she be both? Funny, at that particular moment she didn't know. All her life she felt incomplete. Now she knew why? She hated thinking that her mother had deliberately deceived her all these years. And what had forced their hands tonight? Bronze was angry—hurt.

The telephone rang. She let her machine answer. It was Stephanie.

"Bronze, if you're home, please pick up." She paused for a moment. "Okay, honey, call me when you get in. I'll be up."

Bronze wanted to pick up the phone, but something held her back. It was the memory of a little girl asking about her father and seeing her mother collapse in tears. That little girl still lived in Bronze's heart.

The phone rang again. It was Brandon. "Did you forget about me? I'm at Ebony's and you're not. I thought we were meeting for drinks."

"Brandon, I can't talk now. I'm not in the mood tonight."

"What's wrong?"

"I gotta go." She started crying again.

"Bronze, talk to me. What's going on?"

"Good-bye, Brandon." She hung up.

Fifteen minutes later, he was at her door.

"Brandon, I told you."

"I'm not leaving until you tell me what's going on."

She let him in, shaking her head as he made himself comfortable on the couch.

"I'm here for you, Bronze. Now what's wrong?"

Unable to hold back the tears any longer, she found herself telling Brandon the story of her parents' courtship and divorce, and how she had been deceived.

Brandon held her for a moment trying to console her. "Bronze, I know you're hurting now, but it's not the end of the world. You'll feel better tomorrow after a good night's sleep. Trust me."

"What? You act like I just skinned my knee or something. Oh, I forgot. Your parents have been married for thirty years. How could you possibly understand what I'm going through?"

"Of course I understand, Bronze. I just think you're overreacting. These things happen all the time."

"But not to Brandon Wilde!"

"Oh, grow up, Bronze. Stop acting like a child. Welcome to the *real* world."

"You know what? I should have known that you couldn't give me what I need."

"Oh, and my bisexual cousin can? At least now I know where your portrait came from."

"What?"

"You heard me. Have you been fucking Julian?"

"Who told you that?"

"Don't worry about it. Just answer my question."

"You're in no position to talk to *me* about being unfaithful. Refresh my memory, Brandon. What was the name of that video you and Capricia starred in?"

"Oh, so you used my cousin to get back at me?"

"Don't flatter yourself. You must really think you're all that."

"So did you fuck Julian?" It was really eating at Brandon. He had to know.

"Wait a minute. I'm having a crisis, and that's all you can think about?"

"Bronze, I need to know."

"Why? Don't you trust me, Brandon?"

He just glared at her.

"That's what I thought. What are we doing together, Brandon. I don't trust you, and you don't trust me." She slowly removed her engagement ring, reached for his hand, placed the ring in his opened palm, and closed it gently. Bronze and Brandon both realized it was over. They embraced one last time before saying good-bye.

Bronze felt the sudden urge to get away from it all, to go someplace where she could be alone and think. Maybe to the Bahamas. Someplace where she could lie on the beach and melt her troubles away in the sun or at least forget about them temporarily. She needed to get her head together. Adam Malone was her father. Her thoughts returned to the weekend in D.C. when they had first met. She remembered how relaxed and comfortable she had felt sharing her feelings with him and the ease with which they had spoken. It all seemed so natural. In retrospect, it was eerie—the familiarity of their spirits.

Bronze prepared for bed knowing full well that she'd be unable to sleep. By one in the morning she was still wide awake. Her mind was racing. She knew that sleep would be her only freedom, but it just would not come. Then she sat up in bed suddenly remembering her grandmother's remedy for insomnia. She flicked on the lamp and took the Bible from the nightstand, holding it to her chest. She couldn't remember the last time she had picked it up other than to dust her furniture. She opened it to the one hundred and twentieth Psalm. "In my distress I cried unto the Lord and He heard me." If ever she needed the Lord, it was now.

Bronze kept the Bible turned to the scripture and gently placed it on the pillow next to her. Within the next half hour she was sound asleep, waking only once during the night.

Sunday morning Bronze awakened with a strong desire to attend church. It had been months since she had actually gone, but this particular morning she wanted to hear the word of God.

She showered and dressed for Mt. Zion's eleven o'clock service. It was the first time in she didn't know how long that she hadn't called her mother in the morning. It wasn't that she wanted to punish Stephanie, it was just that she didn't know what to say to her.

The large congregation was typically attired in all their finery. Normally, Bronze would have been right there with them, but not this morning. It all seemed so trivial and unimportant.

As she sat in a rear pew, Bronze looked around. She recognized many of the members of the congregation, and they in turn nodded or smiled in her direction. She almost stood when they welcomed the visitors. It had been so long since she'd attended church.

Elder Darden's sermon was on forgiveness. Bronze listened with only half an ear, as this was not what she wanted to hear. She could not find it in her heart to forgive either her mother or father just yet. The wounds were too fresh. It seemed strange referring to Adam as her father.

Elder Darden paused for a moment, and Bronze listened with her heart. "I'm telling you that grudges and anger eat away at your soul until there's nothing left. Well they're tricks of the enemy. But there's freedom in Jesus Christ. Ask the Lord to help you to forgive. No matter what the problem. He is able. If God can forgive us our transgressions, then certainly we must follow his example. Whether it's mother, father, sister, brother, neighbor, or friend, learn to forgive.

Can I get a witness? I said, can I get a witness?" Members of the congregation shouted amen and threw up a hand.

Bronze did not wait for the altar call. Instead, she slipped out and drove to her mother's. When she arrived, Stephanie was still in her bathrobe drinking vanilla latte. She watched her daughter come through the door not knowing what to expect.

Bronze broke the ice by embracing her. Neither of them spoke, tears intermingling on their cheeks.

"Ma," Bronze said, releasing her mother, "I need to get away for a few days. I need some time to think. Time to get my head together. Can you understand that?"

"Of course I do, sweetheart. Where will you go?"

"I'm not really sure. Maybe the Bahamas."

"Just let me know when you'll be leaving." She embraced her daughter. "You know I love you, Bronze, and I raised you the best way I knew how."

"I know, Ma."

Chapter 39

Three days later, Bronze was on an airplane bound for the Bahamas. She had taken a week's vacation from Hubert's and was delighted at how relaxed she was already beginning to feel. Thanks to her portable CD player and a few fashion magazines, the flight was a short one. After she landed, it seemed to take forever to get from the airport to the hotel.

The hotel itself was situated on the beach, and her room overlooked the Caribbean Sea. She preferred this small, quaint hotel to the large five-star one up the street. She glanced out the eastern window, mindful of the activity below. There were a few studs and voluptuous women on the sparsely populated sands. Even a nude sunbather or two. Apparently, the pool was the hotspot that day with its three swim-up bars.

Since it was only two in the afternoon, Bronze had plenty of time to get reacquainted with the sun. She peeled off her clothes, donned a coral one-piece bathing suit, and grabbed her straw tote bag. Opting for the beach to be alone with her thoughts, she spotted an empty reclining lounge chair. She loved the smell of the sea. And the closer she got to the shore, the more eager she was to dive into those crystal-clear turquoise waters. It was invigorating.

She returned to the lounger and proceeded to massage the suntan lotion into her skin. Soon, she was in another world as her body absorbed the tunes from her Discman. She fell asleep in the sun, and when she woke up it was dinnertime.

Bronze took a quick dip in the water before heading back to her room. She lay on the bed, her mind returning to the circumstances surrounding her birth. She rationalized that when a baby is brought into the world, there is one guarantee: It has both a mother and a father. It just didn't seem fair that she had been deprived of that basic element. Fresh tears spilled onto her cheeks. She felt so inadequate. Frankly, she wondered if she would have been better off left in the dark. They say ignorance is bliss. Was knowing better than not knowing? Was the truth always the best policy? She had her doubts.

Bronze shampooed, showered, and prepared herself for dinner. She slipped into a lime-green romper and sandals. Bronze ate alone in the outside dining area, with only her thoughts for company.

She couldn't understand how Adam Malone could just abandon her without thinking twice. Didn't he have a conscience? What kind of man would forsake his own flesh and blood for his career? Bronze wondered if Adam had ever given her a second thought throughout the years. Had he ever tried to contact her? Had he ever reached the point where he wanted to renege on his promise to Stephanie? Did she have brothers and sisters floating around? Somehow, Bronze thought not. But she did have a whole other family somewhere: grandparents, aunts, uncles, cousins. Did they know of her existence? Would they accept her into the fold? There were so many unanswered questions.

But the most important issue with which Bronze was faced, was how to heal herself. Her self-esteem had been badly bruised, and her self-image was warped. She didn't have all the answers, but she knew she needed time. She silently prayed that the Lord would see her through this ordeal. *Lord, please don't forsake me in my hour of need the way I've forsaken you.* She had been unfaithful to God. And now she was like a drowning man, grabbing on to anything to avoid going under. She was desperate. Would God understand? Then again, she reasoned, maybe it took a personal crisis to call on God. In any event, Bronze decided to hold on to her mustard-seed faith. It was all she had left.

The next morning she slept in and ordered a big breakfast of bacon and eggs, waffles, and coffee. She was famished. She decided to treat herself to a full-body massage that afternoon. She could use a stress reliever. In the meantime, she headed to the pool for a quick dip and then decided to lay out in the sun, her skin enjoying its deliciousness. She dozed off and nearly missed her appointment.

The masseuse was a young, Bahamian woman named Marla. She was petite, but her hands were strong, yet soft. She gave Bronze the treatment from head to toe, kneading her skin and working out all the kinks. Bronze loved every moment of it. Next, Marla covered her skin with a seaweed scrub. She guided Bronze into the shower where she instructed her to rinse thoroughly and then return to the table for the final phase of the massage.

Bronze floated back to her room feeling like a million bucks. She drifted off to sleep, awakening in time for a late dinner. She ordered the lobster and shrimp platter, saving room for dessert. She splurged on German chocolate cheesecake. It was absolutely decadent.

She finished her meal and decided that a moonlit walk along the beach, would suit her just fine. It was a beautiful evening. All around her were couples. Couples in love. Her thoughts drifted to another couple—Stephanie and Adam.

As her plane taxied down the runway, Bronze checked her seat belt to make certain she was securely buckled in. She thought about home. Bronze was beginning to realize that Stephanie and Adam were not perfect, but at least she'd been conceived in love. Maybe they hadn't made the best decisions, but Stephanie had only been trying to shield her daughter from the truth, which Stephanie didn't quite understand so, how could she expect her child to?

Chapter 40

Adam entered his Middle Heights suite, closed the door behind him, and looked around. His eyes riveted to the fully stocked bar and the king-size bed, both of which he was in dire need. He removed his jacket and loosened his tie, laying them on a nearby chair. He headed for the bar and fixed himself a drink.

He was a Hennessy man, preferring it on the rocks. He sipped the tea-colored liquid slowly, letting it slide down his throat. It had been a long day. He headed for the bed to take a load off his feet.

He could see Paige Lawson's headline now: *Full of BS and Her Daddy Too!* He'd be finished, washed up. He had abandoned Bronze for the sake of his career. Now would he be forced to abandon his career for Bronze's sake? It was the irony of life, poetic justice.

He took another sip of cognac. Since Bronze's birth, not a single day went by that he hadn't thought of her. There were so many days, too numerous to count, that he wanted to claim his daughter. Did she resemble him? Did she have any of his habits? Would she forgive him? Would he ever be able to make it up to her? Should he even try?

Adam recalled the dinner in D.C. where they had first met. She was such a lady. He knew her parents had done a wonderful job of raising her and must be quite proud. He remembered thinking how he'd love to have a daughter like her.

Should he drop out of the congressional race? His only other option would be to call a press conference and break the news to the public and the media before Carson and his camp did. Adam did not want to reveal Bronze or Stephanie's identity. He refused to put them through that. But he was certain that Carson wouldn't give it a second thought. Carson was a by-any-means-necessary politician.

Adam drained the glass and set it on the nightstand. He checked his watch. Well, he concluded, there was only one thing to do.

Stephanie sat in the arrival area of the Cleveland Hopkins International Airport, awaiting her daughter's return. She didn't know what to expect. Fear and hope gripped her simultaneously. She checked her watch. The flight was scheduled to land in the next twenty minutes.

She strolled to the newsstand a bought a copy of *Candor,* flipping through it to kill time, her mind racing a mile a minute. Eventually, Bronze's plane landed, and Stephanie immediately rose, as passengers reuniting with family and loved ones, passed by.

Stephanie spotted Bronze coming in to the gate. She was well tanned and did justice to her name. She appeared relaxed. Their eyes met and locked. Finally,

Bronze flashed that familiar smile that Stephanie knew all so well. Stephanie's eyes always lit up when she entered the room. Bronze ran toward her mother and the two embraced—a long, intense hug. For a moment neither of them spoke.

"I missed you, Ma!"

"I'm glad you're back, Bronze. Let's get your bags and go home."

Just like old times, Stephanie had a fresh bag of pastries awaiting her daughter. It never ceased to amaze Bronze how often she permeated her mother's thoughts. Stephanie was always thinking of ways to put a smile on Bronze's face. And she always succeeded.

They made a fresh pot of herbal tea and sat around the kitchen table enjoying each other's company. Stephanie remained quiet watching her daughter, and patiently waiting for Bronze to start the conversation, not wanting her own anxieties to resurface. Finally, Bronze spoke.

"Boy, it's good to be home. Five days in the Bahamas were enough."

"How was it?"

"Great. I had plenty of time to just lie on the beach and think about the three of us. And I realize now that you did what you thought was best. And you did it out of love. I never doubted your love for me, and I'm not gonna start now." Bronze grabbed her mother's hand and squeezed tightly. The tears rolled down both of their faces, but this time they were not tears of anger, fear, or hurt. They were tears of joy.

"I wish I could have come to this conclusion right away, but some things take a little time. I guess being an only child made me self-centered. But it's not always about me. And I want to apologize for being so insensitive and selfish. You've gone through so much and kept it bottled up all these years. I'm sorry, Ma. Forgive me." Bronze reached across the table and hugged her mother tightly.

"I'm the one who should be apologizing to you. It's my fault that you grew up without your father. And that was wrong. I tried to love you enough for the both of us, but I guess I just made a mess of things. I wish I could turn back the clock and do things differently, Bronze."

"Ma, you know what I think? I think that before we were born we were spirits in heaven, and God asked me one day, 'Bronze, who do you want for a mother' and I said 'Stephanie Sutton.' And the Lord said, 'Well, you know, Bronze, it's not always going to be easy. You won't have any brothers or sisters, and many days it'll just be the two of you. Are you sure that's who you want?' And I said yes. Ma, I haven't regretted having you for my mother for one moment in these twenty-six years. And if I had it to do all over again, I would still choose you."

"Oh, Bronze, I love you so much. I'm so blessed to have you as my daughter. You're everything I prayed for and more. Lord, I thank you."

"We're blessed to have each other, Ma."

Through red eyes and swollen lids they were both able to smile. Stephanie got up and returned with a box of tissue. They blew their noses.

"So what's been happening around here since I've been gone?"

"Your friends have been calling—Angela, Julian, even Brandon."

"So wha'ja tell them?"

"I just said you needed to get away for a while."

"Is Adam still in town?" she asked, searching her mother's eyes.

Stephanie nodded.

Bronze hesitated only slightly. "In time we'll talk."